MW01101597

DAWNING POINT

DAWNING POINT

Elizabeth Von Leven

Lutheran Publishing House

National Library of Australia
Cataloguing-in-Publication entry
Von Leven, Elizabeth, 1931-   .
        Dawning point.
        ISBN 0 85910 593 8.
        I. Title.
A823.3

Printed and published by
Lutheran Publishing House,
205 Halifax Street, Adelaide, South Australia   91 – 0615

CHAPTER ONE

'I don't want to have lessons!' Elya shouted. Her sturdy, brown legs carried her swiftly across the grass toward the forest.

'Naughty, naughty, naughty Elya!' sang Chirrik, and the other birds, swooping, beat her lightly with their wings. Elya ran wildly, her small body dodging in all directions. Chirrik, always concerned about the child, dived at her, and tried to turn her back to the crystal pool, where Trefoil, the tree, waited.

'Go away!' cried Elya waving her arms as she ran. It was not the first time she had been defiant, but she usually laughed in fun. This time she was in earnest.

Heedless of the damage she caused, she dodged among yellow flowers growing in the tangled, green undergrowth. Her feet crushed the delicate petals into perfume, and the grass sprang to protect flowers. It prickled her feet, but she took no notice, and searched among their hardy clumps to find a stick. Picking up a broken tree branch, she shouted: 'Stop following me!' She swished the branch around her head.

The birds looked at one another. 'It's no use, use', sang Chirrik. 'Let her alone till she comes to her senses, senses, senses!' She led them away.

Without pausing to see where she was going, Elya ran helter-skelter in the dense forest. She had no idea that she was going west, away from Living Water Country where she lived. She only knew that she was running away from the tree who wanted to make her life dull and boring.

Though Elya had been warned that the forest thinned in the west into dry, dusty saltbush plains which led to an ugly swamp, at this moment she had one thought in her mind. Lessons! Her friend, Rarebit, had told her about lessons, and she believed him.

'Don't ever have lessons, Elya', the rabbit had said. 'They're as dull as dull, an' you'll be dull an' borin' before you know it.'

She forgot that all sorts of dangerous creatures lived in the swamp and might come to this part of the forest occasionally. Besides, she had never met any forest creature who had not been friendly.

Elya had been born in the forest. Her mother and father had been farmers, forest folk glad to live among flowers, birds, and animals who rapidly became their friends. Only when Elya's parents had gone beyond the Great Mountains to the land of Never Return, and their tiny daughter was left an orphan, did the friendship of the forest folk show its true worth, for Elya became their special interest. She thrived under their care. At six years, she was strong and healthy.

She was out of breath when she finally stopped running. Long, dark trees with wooden faces stared at her. She suddenly felt afraid of their rough, brown bark and stiff arms. Though all the trees here had heard of Elya, the small daughter of the dead farmer and his wife, they had never seen her. They were strong, silent trunks, unfriendly to strangers.

'I'm Elya', said the child, but there was no answer.

Elya walked on a few paces, and stopped to look around her. No sign of her pool. No sign of her great tree. She walked slowly under the dark trees. White pebbles rose and fell with a plop in the grass as she kicked her feet along the ground.

'Lauristal's mean!' she grumbled. 'She could have said something to the tree.' Instead, Lauristal the pool, with her crystal drops making rainbows as Elya splashed, had only smiled from her depths. She liked everyone to enjoy her fresh water, but she agreed with Trefoil about lessons.

Elya picked up a stone and flung it at a small tree. The sapling creaked with pain and cracked its twigs.

'O I'm sorry!' Elya said.

The tree waved its leaves.

She sighed. Everything in her part of the forest

6

talked. Of course, she knew Living Water Country was a special land. Trefoil had said those who lived there had gifts. So did the creatures in the lands nearby, if they chose to use them.

Elya's face grew sullen. 'I don't want lessons!' Her voice was sulky in the still air.

'S-s-s-st! Quite right', said an oily voice from a bush nearby. 'I've never had any time for them myself.'

Elya jumped, and stared at the bush. The leaves rustled, and a long, wriggling creature slid into sight. Though snakes were not welcome in Living Water Country, Elya had occasionally seen them near the pool, but she had never seen one like this.

His scaly body had colourful markings, but, as the sun shone on his back, the light disappeared and, around the place where the snake lay, a murky gloom gathered like a cloud of evil. From his mouth came a flame that rose into the air with an odour of stale perfume, faeces, rotting animals, and dirty sweat. And the head! A monster head, with dark, handsome features, features that twisted, sneered, and mocked the world!

'Who're you?' gasped Elya.

'Oh? You don't know me?' mocked the snake. 'I'm Dreevil.' He coiled himself comfortably round a log and looked at her. His beady eyes gleamed with amusement.

Elya was fascinated. 'Are you a snake?' she asked, head on one side, eyes inquiring.

Dreevil writhed his long body, and hissed with laughter.

'Why are you laughing?' Elya was annoyed. The forest creatures, in her part of the forest, laughed with her. They never mocked like this creature.

Dreevil stopped laughing, and stared at her for some moments. Elya felt uncomfortable. 'I'm a friend', he said at last. His eyes glinted.

'Friends care for you, and I've never seen you before', Elya said with conviction.

'Even babes —' muttered Dreevil.

Elya looked at him doubtfully. 'Well', said Dreevil. 'It's time to remedy that, isn't it? I could show you how I care, if you come with me.'

There was something so cunning in his face that Elya felt afraid. 'No, not today, thank you', she said politely.

'Now, don't be backward. You'll never need lessons if you follow me. Come on . . . just follow.'

Elya was fascinated by the snake's swaying head. She shrank from going with Dreevil, creeping creature that he was, but her eyes were held. Try as she might to stay where she was, Elya felt herself being drawn forward as Dreevil slid away.

'No . . . no . . .' she pleaded. Fear made her feel sick.

Suddenly, the sound of crashing through the trees reached her. Elya turned her head, and the spell was broken.

'Elya!' roared a deep voice. 'Where are you?'

'Rowlie!' exclaimed Elya, delight and relief on her face. The snake slid out of sight as the great, muscular form of a lion came into view.

'What're you doing here?' growled the lion, shaking his tawny mane. 'I saw you running away. Don't you know this part of the forest is dangerous?' He stopped growling as he became aware of Elya's white face. 'What happened?' he asked.

'There . . . there was a snake . . .' Elya began to cry.

'With a big head?'

Elya nodded. Scowling, Rowlie padded around trees and bushes. He searched carefully, but there was no sign of the creature.

'I didn't know Dreevil came so far!' Rowlie exclaimed. He puckered his forehead. Sometimes he was slow, but not where Dreevil was concerned.

'Elya', he said as he returned to the child, 'you need lessons. The forest creatures can't always protect you. You want to be able to recognise Dreevil and his tricks.'

Tears flowed down the child's cheeks. She ran to the lion and, putting her arms around his huge head, buried her face in his thick, furry coat.

8

'Come', growled Rowlie gently. 'Sit on my back, and I'll take you home.'

Elya did as she was told. As he padded toward the log cabin, the lion sang cheerfully:

'Plod, plod, plodding along,
All the earth is alive with a song.
Homeward, homeward, just you and me,
With a growl and a rowl and a roaring so free.
Roo-ar, roo-ar, rooo-aaar!'

He opened his mouth wide at the last line and made so much noise that the baby rabbits, not yet at school because they were too small, scampered away to hide behind tufts of grass. With startled eyes, they peered at him as he passed.

In the distance, Elya could see Magis, the river, rushing through the meadow to the sea in the south. She glimpsed the wide expanse of blue water glimmering among the trees. 'The sea looks as though it is waving to the Great Mountains', she said.

Rowlie turned his big head to look at the mountains, their topmost points in mist and rosy light. He shook his mane as though he, too, greeted them. Magis the river had his source in the Great Mountains, and all the forest creatures in Living Water Country knew that Magis brought life and blessings from the north.

Before long, the lion, with his small burden, reached the pool.

Elya slid off Rowlie's back and, with wide, dark eyes, looked up at the tree who had watched over her all her life in place of her parents. Trefoil was old, aged above all other trees, and as wise as he was old. In spite of his crusty appearance, Elya knew he had a kind heart that melted to tenderness at times.

'Dreevil', said Rowlie briefly. Trefoil and Lauristal looked at one another in concern.

Rowlie was making the most extraordinary faces, rolling his yellow eyes, and twisting his face into such weird expressions, that the pool wrinkled in mirth. Trefoil had been prepared to scold the child, but Rowlie made him chuckle.

'So, Elya', he said in his pompous, precise way. 'Are you so frightened of me that you had to run away?'

'No', said Elya. 'I love you, Trefoil.' She ran to the tree and flung her arms about his strong trunk. The lion was pleased. He rumbled as he moved away.

Trefoil rustled his leaves. 'Well, my dear, let us have some balance. Tell me, what is so bad about lessons?'

Elya drew away and put her hands behind her back. 'I'll never be able to play with my friends or wash in the pool . . . or anyfink!' she said miserably.

'Speak correctly, Elya. The word is "anything". And what you say is nonsense. Lessons are only part of everyday. You will have time for friends, of course. And no-one would dream of stopping you from swimming in Lauristal or listening to Magis. If you work hard and pay attention, I shall be able to give you holidays.'

'But Rarebit says . . .'

'Rarebit would', interrupted Trefoil grimly. 'He follows that hare around and copies him. That is the extent of his lessons. Anything else would be too much trouble for that rabbit.'

'But he's my special friend', said Elya.

'Yes, yes.' Trefoil sighed. 'Very well, leave Rarebit aside. Elya, you are a human being. Trees and flowers and animals have their own lessons from parents. Chirrik teaches her young to fly; Rowlie gives his cubs a great box over the ears when they roll around too much. They learn to growl and hunt like lions. You have been having lessons ever since you were born, but inside you there is a wealth of knowledge that must be given its chance to grow. You can keep on living without it, if you wish, but your life will be so much poorer.'

Elya's black eyes were fixed on him. She only half understood what he was saying, but he sounded so much in earnest that she listened carefully.

'There must be balance', said the tree, drawing breath at last.

'Elya', said Lauristal gently, 'don't be foolish! We love you, and we only want what's best. If Rowlie hadn't gone to look for you today, would you have known what to do?'

Elya's face clouded at the thought of the snake. Suddenly, she lit up with mischief and, before Trefoil could stop her, she dived into the pool.

'Naughty Elya!' scolded Chirrik. 'Wasting time! Get out, out, out!' She swooped down and pretended to peck the child.

Elya giggled.

'And what's so funny, funny, funny?' demanded the bird.

'You look funny when you're cross.' Elya laughed. The bird did look comical with her flustered feathers and fussy manner. Chirrik's day had not been a good one, and, when she dived at Elya this time, there was purpose in the swoop.

'Naughty, naughty, naughty!' she screamed.

Elya rolled out of the pool to escape, and put her hands over her head to protect herself. The crystal drops dribbled over her skin and fell like sparkling gems on the ferns at her feet.

'Sorry, sorry, sorry', she said laughing, and Chirrik, satisfied that the child was doing as she was told, flew off in a flurry of feathers.

Elya dried herself quickly in the long grass. 'Please, Trefoil, can't I begin lessons tomorrow?' she begged. 'Please!'

Trefoil looked at her thoughtfully. 'Yes, tomorrow', he said at last.

Elya, with a brilliant smile, scampered away, but not too far. She kept closer to the tree and the pool than she usually did, and once or twice she looked at the forest and shivered.

'We must plan lessons immediately', Trefoil said to Lauristal. 'Tonight while Elya is asleep, I shall call a special meeting of the assembly, and we shall discuss ways and means.'

The water swirled on Lauristal's beautiful face. The pool could scarcely remember the time she came into being. One day, as Magis the mighty river had swelled after a shower of rain, he flooded the land around him for many miles. Some of his water was captured in a circle of rocks, but instead of withdrawing it as he swished by, Magis had paused and smiled. The pool pleased him. She was peaceful and calm, a perfect place for forest creatures to drink his healing waters. He allowed the pool to remain, and every day sent some of his water by a rivulet that fell in a waterfall over his rocks, travelled a short distance across the meadow, and dropped gently into the pool beside a cluster of laurel trees. Magis called the pool Lauristal.

CHAPTER TWO

Elya laughed and played, romped and swam, until night once again touched the meadow. She appeared to have forgotten the snake, but when it was time for her to return to the log cabin where she lived, she was only satisfied when Rowlie, the great lion, with the comical, ordinary face and huge muscles, had sniffed every corner.

As usual, the animals had swept and tidied the cabin. They had taken it in turns to do this chore since Elya was a baby. A new grass dress, the work of her friends the birds, was hanging in the corner. On the table were bowls heaped with nuts, fruit, and delicious tirips leaves from the health plant that grew only in Living Water Country, and which was the main food of all the forest creatures. One bowl held fresh milk.

By the work of his hands, her father had made the cabin and everything in it. Her mother had made the soft down coverlet which the animals shook every day, and left in the sun before they put it back on her bed. The animals had plumped her grass mattress, too.

Bed was inviting, but all the same, until the lion promised he would guard the door, Elya felt she could not eat or sleep. However, when Rowlie lay across the front step, and laughed in rolling growls each time she peeped through the slit that served as a window, she settled at last. She ate her meal slowly with her eyes half closed and her head nodding. A few minutes later, she stretched on her soft bed, and the perfume of sweet, dried grass and roses lulled her to sleep.

As soon as it was dark, Trefoil sent the messenger breeze to gather the forest councillors at the side of the pool.

Rowlie the lion, replaced at the cabin doorstep by one of his sturdy sons, was the first to arrive.

A short time afterwards, Tricko the fox, with his big bushy tail sweeping the ground as it had so often swept Elya's cabin, loped into the clearing. His light brown eyes were intelligent and wise. Some would have said he was cunning, but Tricko had grown beyond that. His cunning had gone with his youthful follies, and he had become an animal of great insight.

Next came Haro the hare. Most of the forest creatures respected Haro because he planned so well. There was, however, something unusual about him. He stood apart at first, as though he was better than the other creatures. He almost sneered at them. Rowlie appeared ordinary beside him, but the lion's sturdy honesty made him trustworthy and appealing.

Behind Haro trotted Rarebit the rabbit, an unusual little creature with round, chubby face, big blue eyes, unlike other rabbits, and attractive manners. He was older than he appeared, and was part of the assembly because he often played with Elya. Trefoil thought it might make him responsible, but, all the same, the rabbit kept close to Haro for security.

Chirrik was there with other birds and insects and many more of Elya's friends. Elya would have been delighted to see them all together, but this was business and no place for a child. Because the clearing was already crowded, Trefoil asked the breeze to carry messages from every corner of the forest, so that everyone who was interested in Elya could take part in the discussion.

Everyone loved Elya except Dreevil, but Dreevil lived in the swamp, not in Living Water Country, which he despised. His friends were wicked, ugly creatures. Few of them ever came to take the healing waters. The forest creatures knew little about the inhabitants of the swamp or Saltbush Plains. They knew Dreevil and his evil ways, and they knew the danger to those who followed him. They taught their children how to deal with him so that life would be happy and safe.

'H-m! H-m!' Trefoil called all the chattering creatures to attention. 'As you know, you have been gathered here to plan Elya's future.' The tree, in honour of the occasion, had polished his leaves to a dignified sheen. He plunged into the main subject without wasting time. 'You have heard, of course, about the incident with Dreevil this afternoon. Elya has reached the age when she needs lessons. She will not always be able to lean on her forest friends.'

There was a murmur of agreement.

'There will be a time', continued Trefoil, 'when she is called to go on the quest. We all have to face it in different ways. She will then leave the forest. She must be prepared.'

'Surely, Trefoil, life itself teaches the best lessons.' Haro looked wise. He stroked his brown and white fur.

Lauristal rippled her waters. 'Elya, as yet, knows so little of life.'

'Life and the quest go together', said Trefoil. 'Elya has no parents to guide her. We have all taught her, but head knowledge is one thing, and heart knowledge, making us ready for the quest, is something quite different.'

'You're not the only one who knows that', interrupted Haro. He preened himself and twitched his nose.

Trefoil regarded him steadily. 'That is why I called you all together', he said at last. 'We must all play our part.'

'But it's fitting, Trefoil', said Lauristal, 'that you're her main teacher. You've protected her so well all these years.' She avoided looking at the frowning hare.

'Yes, yes', agreed the forest creatures. 'Trefoil, of course.'

Haro said nothing. His eyes bulged, but there was no expression on his furry face. 'Thank you, friends, for your trust', said Trefoil, stretching his great, polished trunk until it shimmered white in the moonlight. 'She will need lessons in many things.

15

The wisdom of the forest.' All the creatures knew that Trefoil had wisdom in plenty.

'Tenderness, love and care.' Trefoil looked at Lauristal, where these qualities shone most brightly.

'Strength.' His gaze turned to Rowlie.

'Ways to outwit Dreevil.' Trefoil actually smiled at Tricko. The fox chuckled and lowered his brown eyes.

'O come now, Trefoil', interrupted Haro. 'You don't think Dreevil is interested in a mere child, do you?'

The fox rubbed his red-brown fur. His clever face was pointed and angular in the shadows. 'Dreevil is interested in everyone', he said quietly. 'Even hares', he added slyly.

Haro's ears wiggled with annoyance. He was about to retort, when Trefoil's old branches waved them to silence.

'Whatever is true about Dreevil', he said, 'Elya must be prepared for her call, and she must learn that following her own way is dangerous'.

'Exaggeration!' sniffed Haro.

'But it's true, true, true', sang Chirrik.

A flush of irritation crossed the hare's face. He was not used to the forest creatures disagreeing with him. Rarebit, trying to comfort him, snuggled against him, but the hare roughly pushed him aside.

'Perhaps she needs awareness most of all', Rowlie said with a great joyful laugh to change the subject.

Trefoil nodded. 'As Rowlie says, awareness helps us recognise the call in the first place. We will be given the courage to follow, when the quest is known. Only the Great Mountains hold the secret.'

The forest folk sat quietly reflecting, but Haro, bad-tempered and humiliated, muttered under his breath: 'Stuff and nonsense!'

Rarebit heard him, and tumbled over with laughter, not because he thought it funny, but because he wanted to please the hare, and it must be said that Haro warmed to the rabbit more than he had done before.

At last the animals went home, and silence reigned in the land.

Out of the night, Dreevil, shiny back reflecting the moonlight, slid into the clearing. He gazed at the log cabin. Slowly, slowly, he moved through the grass, and shivered as the dew-swept blades brushed his body. Slowly, slowly, he slithered carefully, O so carefully, his eyes fixed, every sense alert.

Suddenly he stopped. A shadow moving around the log cabin darkened his view of the doorway.

'S-ss-st!' he hissed. The sound was a mere whisper.

Rowlie stood at the door of the log cabin and peered into the darkness.

The snake dropped low in the grass as a low growl rose into the night. Through the tufts of grass, the snake saw the lion open his huge mouth and yawn. Great teeth gleamed in the moonlight. The snake shuddered.

The lion, listening intently, stood for some minutes. Finally he turned and padded to the other side of the cabin.

With a flash of silver, the snake whipped around and regained the shelter of the forest.

Chirrik called restlessly in her sleep, and tucked her head under her wing.

Dreevil slid toward the swamp.

CHAPTER THREE

Next day, when Elya skipped to the pool, the tree said firmly: 'Lessons, Elya. We begin now.'

The child nodded.

As usual, Trefoil wasted no time. He gave Elya a garden plot which Tricko had prepared during the night, and, while showing her how to plant seeds, he named them all.

Elya began to enjoy herself. With dirty face, she pottered around happily, and planted brown, white, and yellow seeds in the black earth. Trefoil taught her to weed, plant, and weed again. She must water the seeds every day except when it rained, he said. 'Not too much water, you understand. Otherwise, you will drown the seeds and they will not grow . . . There must be balance.'

The sun was high in the sky when he sent her away. 'Lesson time is over', he said.

Elya lingered.

'Free time', said Trefoil firmly. 'There must be balance.'

In the following days, Elya often heard him say: 'There must be balance'. It was his motto. Sometimes her black eyes sparkled as Trefoil explained his lesson in that precise, dry way of his, and when she guessed the words were coming she said it with him: 'There must be balance'. And she laughed and clapped her hands.

Years went by. As Elya grew, her plants grew with her. By the time she was ten years old, the small plot had spread to her cabin door. She had learnt to plan, so the clearing from the cabin door to the pool was divided into sections of lawn and beds of massed flowers. Her last project had been a vegetable garden, where she planted wild strawberries, greens, and herbs, as well as many varieties of the tirips plant. Fruit trees shaded the garden from the heat of the summer, perfumed the air with blossoms on spring days, and coloured the earth with their leaves in autumn.

By means of the garden, Trefoil taught Elya many lessons of the spirit. He used every new plant and every change of season to find living riches for the child. Elya herself worked so long and tended her garden so carefully that he often had to say: 'Elya, go and play. We must have balance', and Elya, with reluctance, would obey.

Often, Elya would sit on Trefoil's roots and question him. One day, she asked: 'Why does that beautiful rose have to drop its petals and become ugly?'

'The rose is beautiful in her ugliness too', said Trefoil. 'If she did not die, there would be no room for another rose to live. As she dies, another is born.'

'What happens to her?'

'She lives again in the new rose. She always lives, because her beauty has touched you, me, Lauristal, and many others. She lives in our memories.'

'Does everyone live in the memory of everyone else?' asked Elya.

The tree nodded. 'Some more than others, of course.'

'You will live in me because you teach me so many things', said Elya thoughtfully, 'but will I live in you, even when I grow old?'

'No-one more so. There is a special bond between teacher and pupil.' Trefoil's branches quivered with emotion.

'You old tree!' Elya said, and patted his trunk. She had learnt much about life. Her quick mind opened her to Trefoil and Lauristal's example.

'And what about Dreevil?' she asked, her face darkening. One meeting with the snake monster had made an indelible impression.

Trefoil paused. 'He too will live with you', he said at last, 'but only as far as you allow him to influence you, can he harm you . . . It is all a matter of awareness, you see.'

Elya shook her long, black hair from her face. She was puzzled. These lessons were hard, just as Rarebit had told her years ago. 'Awareness?' she queried.

Trefoil's leaves shook in his effort to reach her mind. 'When you open yourself to something', he said, 'it soaks into you, whether it is good or bad. Blue skies, living water, your garden, all kinds of beauty have become part of you during your lesson time. You have been cooperative. But if you refuse to allow something to enter your heart, it does not soak in. That is how it should be with Dreevil. The less you think of him the better. Give him the least notice possible.'

Elya wrinkled her forehead. She thought for a moment. 'He's not worth the trouble', she said with conviction.

Trefoil's roots rattled in the ground. 'Precisely', he chuckled. Lauristal rippled with him.

'She is coming on well', he said, grinning with pleasure. 'Run away and play, Elya. Have a holiday to celebrate. We must have —'

'— balance!' shouted Elya, dancing with glee. She fled along the path calling: 'Rarebit! Rarebit! I've got a holiday!'

The round-faced rabbit hopped up from behind the bushes where he had been lazing in the sunshine. He ran toward her.

'Is it a good idea?' asked the pool.

'You mean the rabbit, I suppose', replied Trefoil. 'No, I am not sure it is. He is a weak creature, but Elya enjoys his company. I do not know why. He does not appeal to me, but there is no actual reason why she should avoid him. He is lazy and silly, certainly, but that has no effect as far as I can see.'

But Elya was influenced by Rarebit far more than the tree knew. She liked the silly, charming creature who enjoyed life so much, and was never serious about anything.

'Why're you workin' so hard?' he asked Elya on this occasion.

'It's important for me to learn', she answered, repeating what Trefoil had so often told her.

'Why?' asked Rarebit.

'Because it is', said Elya, hoping to end his questions.

Rarebit shrugged. 'Just stopped mine', he said. 'I pretended to be too silly to understand, an' they gave up on me. I'm all right. I've just grown. Never have to work like you, poor thing. It's a free life. Play all day.'

'But don't your parents mind?' asked Elya.

'Ran away from home ages ago. Like bein' by myself.' Elya made no comment.

'Well, what do you want to play?' asked Rarebit. 'Hoppity-kick?' Rarebit liked hoppity-kick, because it required no brain work, and he always won. It was a simple game consisting of three hops and a kick repeated until they were tired. The one who remained standing the longer was the winner. At first Elya thought it was a silly game, but the rabbit was so funny when he kicked, that she never failed to laugh until the tears ran down her face.

Time passed quickly and, when the game was over, Elya asked Rarebit to help her collect some tirips leaves. He was greedy, she knew, but she was surprised when Rarebit, while her back was turned, ate more than he picked. They were her plants, after all. When she looked at the rabbit, he returned her gaze steadily with his eyes wide open.

Elya forgave him. There was always plenty of food in the cabin. Even now, when she was older and expected to do her own cleaning, the animals and birds always made sure she had plenty to eat.

Rarebit thought she should refuse to do the cleaning, but Elya liked to keep her cabin as tidy as it was in the old days. It was only fair, when she had been given so much care all her life. She swept and dusted, aired and made her bed, polished the wooden boards and scanty furniture until everything shone. She was proud of her house.

'What're you doin' tomorrer?' asked Rarebit.

Elya laughed. 'I've had a holiday today. I can't expect another one tomorrow.'

'Ninny!' Rarebit said scornfully. 'Lettin' everyone run your life for you! No freedom. That's your trouble.'

'But I need to learn. Lauristal says —'

'Lauristal! If it's not Lauristal, it's Trefoil! I was at the 'ssembly, remember? You're in a bind. Haro says there are other ways of learnin'.'

'What do you mean?' Elya asked.

'Never mind. You're too ignorant to understand. I just think you're a great big silly, an' I think it's all stuff and nonsense!' Rarebit was imitating Haro, whom he admired so much. 'Who wants to learn, learn, all the time? Well, I'll go by myself!'

'Go where?' Elya was curious.

'Bubblin' Springs.'

'Bubbling Springs! I've always wanted to go there! Tricko says he'll take me one day.'

'I'll take you tomorrer', promised the rabbit.

'Couldn't you wait until the next holiday?' begged Elya.

'Nope. It might be rainin'. I hate rain. Tomorrer, or wait for Tricko.'

'I'll come then', said Elya with a deep breath. 'But we'll have to go early . . . I'll run out the back way to avoid Lauristal and Trefoil.'

'Attagirl!' cheered Rarebit, his chubby cheeks glowing. 'We'll have fun!'

Elya felt guilty that night as she made her preparations. She was restless as she stood on Magis's banks and gazed at the living water. Perhaps Bubbling Springs would revive her spirits. All the same, she wished she could go with the approval of Lauristal and Trefoil. No use asking them. They were sure to say No, and she wanted so much to go with Rarebit. Sadly, she walked back to her cabin.

'Tired', said Lauristal, and Trefoil nodded.

'We'll have easier lessons tomorrow', he said.

But when tomorrow came, there was no Elya. Trefoil waited for a time, and then sent Chirrik to find her. The bird returned with the news that

Rarebit and Elya were on the way to Bubbling Springs. 'And if she meets Dreevil, it's her own fault, fault, fault!' added Chirrik, cross that her busy day had been interrupted.

Trefoil was annoyed. 'Here I am giving up my time for a wayward child', he said to the saplings standing near him. 'And what does she do? She keeps me waiting, and upsets my program for the day. Well, I am not sending anyone to fetch her. She must take the consequences of her actions! No balance there! None at all!' He shook his big branches in anger. A shower of leaves fell on the heads of Elya's flowers.

The saplings looked at him, and wisely said nothing. Birds flew from his branches and stayed in other trees for the day. Even Lauristal was quiet. The flowers smiled at one another. Trefoil in a bad mood was a sight!

'Poor little Elya!' murmured one of the saplings.

Trefoil heard him. 'Since Elya has seen fit to play truant', he said stiffly, 'you will do extra work instead'.

Trefoil was teaching the saplings to stand straight and tall, and fear nothing. There were times when growth would be difficult, he said, but all growth was a struggle to something better. Usually Trefoil inspired them so much that they would lift their young branches, look at their new tips shining in the sun, and resolve to do all they could to grow.

Today, however, the tree was grumpy and the lesson dull. With solemn faces, the saplings drilled for hours, until they were bored beyond measure. More than once they wished the lesson was over, and when the sun began to lower itself to rest beyond the forest, and they were finally told they could stop, they were so tired that their leaves drooped.

Then they heard a sound, though it was still in the distance — trees crashing, huge feet trampling, breaking boughs; splintering, crackling, stamping!

'What is happening?' Trefoil was startled from his bad mood.

A flurry of birds overhead and a swift swish of wings answered him. Screeching, they flew in circles round the clearing. Lauristal looked up anxiously. 'Has anything happened to Elya?' she asked, but the question was lost in the noisy babble. The birds bumped into each other in their excitement, and squawked in a crescendo as the noise from the forest increased.

Trefoil, grumpy and worried all day, suddenly lost his temper. 'Will someone tell me what this is all about?' he roared. The forest creatures, including the birds, were shocked into silence, but the crashing boughs and screaming continued, and was now close to the pool.

'Horses!' screeched a bird. 'They're stampeding!'

'Horses?' barked Trefoil. 'There are no horses here!'

The noise was almost on them.

'Quick! Fly, fly, fly!' shrieked Chirrik, and the birds escaped over the tree as three horses, with flaring nostrils and manes tossing wildly, crashed into the clearing. Trefoil could see that they were draught horses, and they were terrified. He had just enough time to gather all his strength into his trunk, when they burst upon him. They kicked their huge hooves and bashed. They wheeled, and neighed, and trampled.

'Elya's garden!' called Lauristal, but it was too late. The horses, wild with fear, ripped it apart under their hooves as they reared, and, falling, galloped again, crushing everything in the clearing. One of the saplings fell to the ground; the flowers were flattened, and Lauristal's water was churned to mud. The poor horses swept from side to side without knowing where to run, or which way to turn.

'Stand still!' thundered Trefoil. Rowlie appeared on the other side of the clearing, and Tricko stood on the opposite bank of the pool. They faced the terrified animals.

The horses reared and screamed. They seemed to be frightened by something behind Trefoil. As the tree twisted, he was just in time to see Dreevil, grinning with delight, lower himself into the grass.

'There is the trouble!' he called. Lauristal, nearly fainting with pain, rippled urgent messages to Magis, and the river roared menacingly. At the sound, Chirrik and her companions returned, and, swiftly diving at the snake, they pecked with sharp beaks at his coiling back. He fought for a time, his poisonous tongue flicking upwards, his eyes red with fury. But the birds were too fierce, and finally Dreevil slid away.

In the meantime, the forest animals, seeing Rowlie and Tricko in danger, joined them. They stood in a circle round the clearing, until the horses became calmer. Lauristal began the lullaby they knew so well:

'Hush to the land near the river of life,

Hush to our worries, hush to our strife.

Lull us to sleep with a lullaby song;

Be with us, Master, all the night long.'

They sang softly, until the horses, feeling the peace, steadied at last.

'Elya's father's horses!' said Lauristal. 'They've been living in the western forest since the farmer and his wife died. They never do anyone any harm. It's Dreevil's work, I'd say.'

'You're right', said one of the horses, shaking his mane. 'He kept shooting darts from that horrible mouth of his!'

The second horse trembled. 'He jumped at us for hours. We panicked!'

'We're sorry for the damage', said the first horse, 'and of course we'll do what we can to fix it . . .'

The garden, wrecked by the huge trampling feet, was scarcely recognisable. Fruit trees were flattened, flowers crushed, bushes splintered! What a sight!

Trefoil looked at the horses. 'Well', he said, 'you certainly need lessons like some of the others. It's a regular school teacher I'm becoming!' Trefoil always pronounced each word distinctly, so to use 'I'm' instead of 'I am' proved how upset he had been.

'If you live near Dreevil you're bound to have trouble. Why don't you stay here?' he asked.

'Yes, why not?' agreed Lauristal. 'There's plenty of grazing near the river.' The pool, with muddy streaks and broken plants around her, tried to popple, but failed dismally.

'Thanks so much', said the first horse gratefully. 'We've often thought of asking, but we didn't like to be nuisances after all these years away from the living water. I'm Naylor, by the way, and this is Winnie, my wife, and my daughter, Colta.'

The other horses looked sadly at the damage they had caused. 'We'd be glad to help', they said.

Trefoil rubbed his bruised trunk. Suddenly he caught sight of Rarebit, who had crept into the clearing and was gaping at Elya's ruined garden. The rabbit had been listening intently to the conversation, and had slowly moved forward until he was almost under the tree. With two strong branches, Trefoil grabbed him and hoisted him high, just as Elya, with horrified face, walked slowly into the clearing.

'The garden', she said. 'O Rarebit, the garden!'

Rarebit was not interested in anything else but his own predicament at that moment. Intermingled fear and defiance crossed his chubby face. He looked at the tree with wide, innocent eyes. Few could resist the charm of those blue eyes, but Trefoil was not in the mood to be charmed.

'What have you to say for yourself?' demanded Trefoil.

The rabbit wriggled in Trefoil's grasp.

The tree held him firmly. 'Well, let me tell you something, young rabbit', he said when Rarebit failed to answer. 'Your lessons are no concern of mine. If you want to waste your time and remain as ignorant as you are, that is no concern of mine, either. Elya, however, is my concern. Her truancy today is a downright lack of balance that will take a month of disciplined learning to correct . . . You . . .' He stopped to give the cringing rabbit a shake. 'If you want to play truant, do it by yourself, and answer to yourself for the consequences. But if I ever find you leading Elya astray again, I shall . . . I shall . . . knock your head off!'

26

He thrust the rabbit away from him, and the little
creature dropped unharmed and rolled over and over
on the muddy grass. Jumping quickly to his feet,
Rarebit ran away as though all the furies of the world
were after him.

Elya, sadness in her dark eyes, wandered from
bruised flower to broken bush. 'So much work lost',
she said. 'O Lauristal, you look dreadful. O I'm so
sorry I went away!'

'Now, child, don't worry about me. No-one could
have prevented the damage. It was too sudden.'
Lauristal's waters circled as though she were crying.

'We're the ones to blame', Naylor interrupted. 'If
we'd known what to do with the snake, this needn't
have happened.'

Elya, heedless of the stranger speaking, sat at Lauristal's side and leant against the trunk of the tree. 'I'm sorry, Trefoil', she said, and put a small brown hand on his roots.

The tree stirred. 'Everyone is sorry', he snapped, 'though I suppose you're sorrier than most since you were not here'. He was feeling his bumps, which did not improve his temper. 'Well, where did you go today?'

'Don't be angry with me, Trefoil. I know I did the wrong thing . . . but the garden's enough punishment.' She began to cry softly, the tears streaming down her face.

Everyone was silent for a time. At last, Elya looked up. 'We went for a picnic to Bubbling Springs', she said with a hiccup. 'It sounded lovely, but it wasn't. Rarebit would run on, and I couldn't keep up with him . . . and I was so tired and dusty and thirsty . . . and the water tasted horrible!' She wept again.

'Bitter-sweet mineral water', proclaimed Trefoil, and Tricko and Rowlie guffawed, while Chirrik warbled with delight.

'It wasn't even pretty', sobbed Elya, 'but you look worse than Bubbling Springs now, Lauristal'.

Lauristal smiled. 'Magis has all the waters in himself', she soothed her.

Tricko, with understanding born of long experience, added quietly: 'Bubbling Springs is well enough in her way. She draws one kind of water, and it's there in case of need, but Lauristal is filled with living water. You'll see. She'll soon be beautiful again.'

Tricko leapt toward the horses who were champing restlessly and feeling ashamed of being the cause of so much trouble. 'Come with me', he said kindly. 'You'll need fresh grass after your ordeal. I hope you'll stay in this part of the forest, or Dreevil may try his tricks again.' He led the horses across the meadow. Rowlie went with him.

The tree looked down on Elya. She was staring blankly at the devastation of her garden. 'O dear! It's hopeless!' Her body slumped. 'It'll never be the same again. Never!' She put her head on her knees. 'O what's the use of lessons?' she muttered.

Trefoil heard her. 'Elya, you made one mistake. Do not make others that are much worse.'

Elya raised her head. Her eyes were swimming with tears, and her black hair hung damply round her flushed face.

'This lesson is much harder than Rarebit ever said it would be', Trefoil continued, his face grim. 'You will need to be brave. You can give up now, of course, and let your garden remain a mess. Or you can pick up the pieces and help your plants grow again.'

The forest was hushed as Elya stood and gazed around her. Leave it? Of course, that would be much easier. But she couldn't bear to let her lovely flowers lie wounded and broken, or watch the bushes, trees, and tirips plants die around her.

'Will you help?' she asked.

'Yes!' cried Lauristal and Trefoil together, and Magis roared with joy.

As the sun set, crowds of the forest animals moved into the broken garden to dance and sing. They offered their help, and even at that time of day, picked up and replanted flowers, shrubs and bushes, though they left the main work until the following morning. There was great rejoicing over the growth of the child. 'She has learnt by her mistake', they said. 'She has courage.' And they sang in a rousing chorus.

Late that night, while Trefoil treated his cuts and bruises, and Lauristal allowed the living water from Magis to heal her wounds and enter her being, Trefoil suddenly thought of something.

'Lauristal', he said, 'where was Haro?'

CHAPTER FOUR

Where was Haro? The tree might well have asked that question.

Haro was sitting under a tree in the forest, taking his ease. He had no intention of involving himself in the horse episode. He was actually pleased that events had turned out as they had. He said to himself: 'Perhaps now those silly forest folk will see that Trefoil is too old to know what he's doing'.

Haro thought that everyone who was old became childish. He could never understand that age can bring great wisdom. In the case of trees, particularly in Living Water Country, wisdom increased day by day with the strength and breadth of their trunks. But Haro would not admit that.

When one of the forest creatures, with more strength of character than most, told him occasionally that he was jealous of Trefoil, Haro always said with a sniff: 'Jealous of an old trunk! What rubbish! I care about the child', and he hopped away.

So, when Rarebit, with his bobtail draggled and his chubby cheeks wet with tears, ran to him, Haro listened while the rabbit sobbed out his story. Haro was furious. His fury was not shown in a normal outburst like other animals. Instead, he stood poised on his hind legs, and wiggled his ears. Otherwise, he neither spoke nor moved, and Rarebit, coming to the end of his tale, stopped crying and looked at him uneasily.

'I knew no good would come of it!' said Haro.

The rabbit was puzzled.

Haro roused himself. 'Trefoil', he explained. 'He's too big for his roots altogether, since he was given responsibility for Elya's education — and too old. Now the horses have done so much damage, perhaps the rest of the forest folk will come to their senses!'

To hide his satisfaction, Haro nibbled the tender grass at his side. A host of insects, tiny silken wings shining in the last rays of the sun, rose around him. He coughed and impatiently brushed them away. 'As for you, you silly rabbit, why do you let him frighten you? He's only a tree; he can't move at all, much less run like you.'

'Just as well', said Rarebit ruefully. 'It was bad enough bein' caught in those strong branches . . . I won't go near him again, Haro, I'm tellin' you!' He cowered at the side of the hare, but sat up suddenly as the insects rose again.

Haro smiled, and his eyes narrowed. 'No', he agreed. 'That wouldn't be wise. You have some sense, Rarebit, after all. We'll teach him a lesson one day, you'll see.'

'Did you see those horses?' Rarebit asked, wide-eyed.

'I saw them racing past', replied Haro indifferently. 'You're wondering why I didn't help, I suppose? All this fuss about a child's garden! What a bore it is! A load of rubbish as far as I'm concerned! Limits freedom!'

Rarebit changed his position and sat on a log. 'That's what I've been tellin' Elya all along', he said earnestly. 'I'm always waitin' round for her to finish lessons.'

'I don't know why you want to have anything to do with her in the first place.' Haro sniffed and sprang to his feet. 'She's only a child, after all, and a very ignorant one at that. But it's up to you, I suppose.'

Rarebit was crestfallen at this criticism. He followed Haro round for the rest of the evening. The hare kept his thoughts to himself, but if Rarebit had been more than a silly rabbit, he would have seen that Haro was plotting something.

Rarebit finally realised that Haro was not listening. He fell silent, and made up his mind that he would stay with the hare, and keep away from Elya and the log cabin in future.

Elya and her friends managed the cabin very well without him. He was far too lazy to help with the cleaning, anyway. The cabin, polished inside and out every day by one of the forest animals, glowed like mellow amber among the trees. Sturdy and solid, it merged with their trunks and became part of them, while Elya's garden, which stretched from the cabin to the pool, was gradually restored to its former beauty.

Every day, Elya looked for the rabbit, and when there was no sign of him she became quieter than she had ever been. Her eyes were sad, but she never spoke about her hurt to any of her friends, not even to Magis when she walked with him each night. She never missed her lessons again, and she listened attentively to every word. But, though she learnt quickly, she would often stop in the middle of her work and gaze through the trees. Trefoil knew she was hoping Rarebit would appear.

The tree, to help her, used all his skill to rouse her interest. Trefoil may have seemed dry and precise, but he was actually a poet versed in the wonder of living things, their growth, their patterns, their beauty, and he spoke with an inspiration peculiarly his own, when he felt the need. 'All the same', he said one night to Lauristal, 'that rabbit should be spanked. He has no right to treat her like this.'

Lauristal sparkled at him. 'Well, you did threaten to knock his head off', she said laughing. 'Don't worry so, Trefoil. Elya is learning. It won't spoil her.'

'Perhaps she is better without the fellow', admitted Trefoil, 'but I cannot help wishing it had happened in some other way. She is losing her childhood before her time.'

A few minutes before, Rowlie had come to the pool for a drink. He blinked at the tree. 'Be patient, Trefoil', he growled. 'Time! It's a great healer. Give her time!'

'Cra-a-ak!' The noise interrupted their conversation. Plop! A bright green frog jumped into the pool, and swam through the crystal-clear water.

'Hello!' Rowlie rolled his eyes at Trefoil. 'A stranger in our midst!' The saplings cracked their young twigs and tittered among themselves.

The frog flopped on a lily leaf and fanned himself. 'Cra-a-ak, cra-a-ak! Glad to find a pool. Needed refreshment', he sighed.

'Ah! One of the green bell frogs from Saltbush Plains', said the tree. 'And what may you be doing in this part of the forest?'

The bell frog stood and bowed. His yellow front skin stretched over his fat stomach as he introduced himself. 'Krakik', he said.

Lauristal rippled with amusement, and Rowlie opened his eyes wide with surprise. His honest face was comically puzzled.

Trefoil was the first to speak. 'Welcome, Krakik', he said with simple dignity.

'Practising to be a singer. Better atmosphere for the voice here.' Krakik stretched his throat, and the shining skin on his head wrinkled as he sang loudly: 'Cra-a-ak, cra-a-ak, cra-a-ak!'

Even the tree smiled at the sound. The frog's black eyes bulged, and his mouth widened so much that it took up two-thirds of his plump body. 'Think it will do', he said with satisfaction. 'Yes. Will do.'

Lauristal looked at Trefoil and Rowlie. She hadn't been expecting a guest, but she was always kind-hearted, especially to those in need. When the tree whispered: 'Well, it can do no harm', she crinkled her waters, and gave the frog one of her best leaves for the night.

She slept restlessly, however. So did the tree. For at odd times Krakik would decide to practise, and 'Cra-a-a-a-k, cra-a-a-a-ak, cra-a-awk!' sounded in the night air with monotonous regularity for half an hour at a time.

In the morning Elya found the frog. He had made a muddy puddle at the side of the pool, and was enjoying himself by wallowing in the dirty water.

'Hullo, Elya', said Krakik splashing mud over the grass. 'Heard of you. Krakik's the name. Here for Forest Festival. Sing, you know.'

33

Elya was delighted. 'You'll make a good playmate', she said.

'S'long as no interference with singing, pleased. Good idea!'

But, when Elya found that the frog came from Saltbush Plains on the edge of the swamp, she was dismayed. 'But . . . but isn't that where Dreevil lives?' she asked. 'In ditches and drains and mud and mess?' Trefoil had told her about the habits of the snake.

'Don't like ditches and drains. Too smelly. Quite partial to a muddy puddle now and then. Good fun. Cwa-a-a-k, cwa-a-ak! Lauristal's best of all. Not murky enough for insects, though.'

'I'll prepare special moss for you', said Lauristal kindly. 'You'll enjoy that. But do move out of the mud. It's not healthy, I'm sure.'

'What about Dreevil?' asked Elya, as the frog, with a kick, landed on a lily leaf, which was muddied and bruised by the impact.

'Cwa-a-ark! Get on with him quite well myself', croaked the frog. 'Not everyone's little darling. Need to deal with him, of course. Cwark! Listening's the worst. Fatal to take notice of him.'

'But when he talks', said Elya remembering, 'you can't help listening. His voice is so smooth it draws you in, somehow.'

'Best not to listen in the first place. Just sing. Doesn't like happy things.'

'I'm happy', said Elya. She danced a few steps in the sunlight and, as the warbling of the birds reached her, she lifted her arms and twirled and whirled to the music, music that lifted her heart to the heavens and brought a light to her face.

Krakik stared at her until she dropped at his side.

'Best to sing', he advised, after looking at her in silence for a few moments. 'Like this. Cr-a-a-a-ak! Cra-a-a-a-a-aak! Cra-a-a-a-a-awk!' He raised his bumpy, green head to the sky, and the air was filled with the ugliest sound Elya had ever heard. None of the brown forest frogs had half the volume. At first she giggled with amusement.

34

'Cwa-a-a-aak, cwa-a-a-a-a-a-ak, cwa-a-a-a-a-ark', sang Krakik in full-throated rasps, his voice rising and falling. He continued until Elya thought he would never stop.

'Does he really think he can sing?' she whispered to the pool.

With all this noise surrounding them, Trefoil wondered what kind of lesson he could give Elya.

'What's the matter with him?' asked Tricko, coming into the clearing. 'I heard the din in the middle of the forest. Is he in pain?'

Elya laughed. 'He wants to be head singer in the forest', whispered Lauristal.

Tricko's face crumpled, and his eyes became yellow with amusement.

'You can't be serious', twittered Chirrik. 'There's not a note of music in it, in it, in it!' She flew to the other end of the clearing, where the sound was muffled.

The gentle Lauristal felt weary. This was only the morning. Somehow, they had to survive the day and avoid hurting their guest's feelings. 'If only he wasn't so loud', she said to Elya.

Trefoil decided that Elya should weed her garden. 'Perhaps it will do instead of lessons, today', he thought. 'The frog will be tired by tomorrow. At least, I hope so.'

However, Krakik croaked at the top of his cracked old voice, and gave no sign of being tired. The noise became worse as time went on, but he persevered. Lauristal's waters were still with exhaustion. No wonder she had a headache!

Hours passed. Elya became irritable, and she snapped at the flowers she tended. 'O it's too much!' she said at last, and threw herself on the grass.

Trefoil agreed. 'You may have the rest of the afternoon to yourself, Elya', he called.

'What did you say?' shouted Elya over the sound of the croaks.

'I said, you may stop now', roared the tree.

At that moment, Krakik ceased practising. 'Mustn't strain it', he said. 'Fine trim at the moment. Better every day. Tip-top soon.' He looked around him. 'Must be lunchtime', he remarked.

Lunchtime had come and gone unnoticed by Krakik. However, Lauristal hastened to prepare a cool meal as she had promised, and soon the frog was stuffing himself with moss pie.

Elya sat on one of Trefoil's roots. 'Aren't you afraid of the snake?' she asked, reverting to the morning's conversation.

'No', said Krakik indifferently. 'Never think of him. One aim in life. Talented. Important to use talents.'

'What makes Krakik think he has talents?' Elya wondered.

'Would you like to play?' she asked. 'Rarebit and I play hoppity-kick sometimes . . . like this.' She jumped up to give a demonstration.

'Sorry', said Krakik when she had finished. 'Upset voice for singing. Too much hopping. Silly game, anyhow. Teach you to sing instead.'

Another lesson was not Elya's idea of fun, but she sat beside the frog.

'Hold hands in front . . . so. Stretch neck . . . That's right. Now, cra-a-a-ak!'

'Cra-a-a-ak!' imitated Elya.

'Fair', said Krakik. 'Now, again.'

By the time half an hour had gone by, Elya was hopelessly bored. Besides, her throat was raspy and raw from imitating the frog. Trefoil and Lauristal, who needed a rest, had long since lost their sense of humour, and the tree drooped beside the exhausted pool. Only the frog enjoyed himself.

'Excuse me', said Elya at last, 'I need some tirips leaves for my throat'. She edged toward the cabin.

'Come with you', said the frog amiably, and hopped beside her until they reached Elya's home. 'Nice cabin!' he remarked as he jumped inside and looked round. 'Good place to sleep. Might do.'

'It's rather dry for you, Krakik', said Elya hastily. No animal ever slept in her cabin, and she certainly didn't want a cold, wet frog. Perhaps he'd try to sleep in her bed! The thought made her shudder.

36

'The doorstep', she suggested quickly. 'That might do. It's always wet underneath, and there's dew in the mornings.'

Krakik hopped outside. There was enough grass and mud underneath the step to make him happy, and Elya tried not to show her relief.

'House should be dampened. Ought to see to it, Elya', said the frog.

Elya felt like telling him to mind his own business, but she remembered what the tree had taught her. 'No need to let others tell you what to feel', the tree said. 'You decide yourself what is right. And', he added, 'it is always better to say nothing than to try to undo what you have said later.' So Elya kept silent.

'Like you!' said the frog suddenly. He blinked at her. 'Not bad looking. Face pale. Too thin by far. Hair straight. Good eyes, though. Clothes . . . well! Not bad at all.'

Elya forgot Trefoil's lesson at that, and she stopped smiling. 'O you old frog!' she said crossly. 'What do you know about anything?'

The frog, offended, hunched his back and turned down the corners of his big mouth. 'Meant to be a compliment', he said.

Elya was not sure whether to laugh or cry. 'What an annoying creature he is', she thought, but she relented.

'Krakik, go somewhere and rest', she said, 'and I'll prepare a party to welcome you . . . just for the two of us'.

Krakik's mouth turned up into a great smile. 'Knew you were first class. Need to relax. See you later.' He jumped off, and for the remainder of the afternoon there was peace in the clearing.

Lauristal sighed when Elya came to draw water and told her what had happened.

'Be careful, Elya', said the tree. 'This is another friendship, like the one with Rarebit, that will demand all your energy, and is bound, at best, to be one-sided.' It was the first time Trefoil had mentioned the rabbit. Elya understood. She flushed.

37

'Politeness always. Friendship sometimes', Trefoil added.

Elya groaned. 'It's difficult. He just attached himself like a limpet, and he's spending the night on my doorstep. I didn't ask him.'

Lauristal chuckled. 'I hope you have a good night, Elya', she said. 'Perhaps we could entertain him in turns.'

Elya grinned, and went cheerfully to the cabin.

As usual, the birds and animals had brought fresh food for the day. Elya prepared for her guest as well as she could, arranging some of the fruit and tirips leaves on the top step outside the cabin, and decorating the makeshift table with pretty flowers and leaves. She was not sure what frogs liked, but Lauristal had given her some of the moss pie that Krakik had enjoyed for his lunch, so at least there was something he could eat, and everyone liked tirips leaves.

Krakik was in the best of spirits when he arrived at dusk. Luckily, he was more interested in the prospect of telling stories about himself than in the food. He had gorged himself in the forest and had slept away the afternoon, so he was full of life and energy.

Elya, lonely for Rarebit's companionship, was fascinated by the frog's tales. Once or twice she thought Krakik was conceited, but his cheerful chatter made up for his weakness.

'Won first prize in the Froggish Festival on Saltbush Plains', he told her. 'Four hundred entries. Lots of good voices. Mine the best. Competing in the Forest Festival for Birds and Animals this time. Bit of practice. Top the lot. Win gold medal.'

At last, Elya became sleepy. She had to be on time for Trefoil's lessons, she told the frog. She said goodnight kindly but firmly, as Lauristal had taught her.

Curling up on her little bed, she prepared for sleep. But it was not to be for some time, for Krakik had decided to have a final practice, and his crawks and craws rose in the clear night air.

Elya tossed and turned. She was glad when Chirrik told the frog 'to keep quiet or else, else, else!' Krakik gave one last defiant 'Cra-a-awk!' and then, to Elya's relief, kept silence. She slept.

'Hs-s-st!'

Elya was awakened by a slithering sound and the slow chuckle that she had never forgotten. Terror flooded her being, and she gripped the sides of her wooden bed with a grasp that pained her fingers. Holding her breath, she hid her face in the soft down of her mattress.

A second later, she heard Krakik's startled 'Cr-r-r-a-ak!' and, raising her head, she strained every muscle and listened for the slightest sound.

'Hss-s-st! Hullo, old friend', Dreevil's oily voice was a breath of poison in the night air.

'Not so much friend', retorted the frog grumpily. 'Frightening people. Crazy! What're you doing here, anyway?'

'Ah, I heard you were here for a very special purpose, my friend, and I came to hear you sing in the Forest Day competition.'

'Not welcome, though', said the frog drily. 'Not with these folk. Living-water folk. Don't like snakes.'

'Ah, but I couldn't stay away from that beautiful voice of yours, and I wanted to see your triumph.' Dreevil's voice dripped with honey. It slid softly into the night, and soothed the ruffled frog.

'Figures!' he muttered sleepily. Krakik was mesmerised by the sound of the smooth voice that continued to lull him into stupor. He was unaware of the glitter in the horrible eyes of the snake, though anyone could have seen it easily, even in the darkness.

'You will sing one day as master of the forest', crooned the snake, and Krakik nodded drowsily. 'You will be great among the great.'

'Cra-awk!' sang Krakik softly, and smiled a wide smile of approval.

Elya, on her bed in the dark cabin, felt herself trembling. She wanted to call: 'Krakik, don't listen! You said yourself he can harm you when you listen!' But her throat closed in terror, and no sound would come through her stiff lips.

The oily voice droned on and on, and still Elya remained frozen in her bed. Why didn't Krakik croak? What was he doing? What was happening?

She realised, suddenly, that Magis had changed his voice. The river rushed and roared like a huge waterfall, and Krakik croaked loudly. All at once, she found she could move. She sprang out of bed and, picking up a piece of wood from the fireplace, raced to the door of the cabin.

Too late! As she opened the door, the moon slid from behind a cloud, and the glade was bathed in silver light just in time for Elya to see Dreevil open his poisonous mouth, and swallow the frog whole. A great wave of cold, clear water rose from the banks of the river and flowed swiftly to the door of the little log house. By the time the water had reached it, however, Dreevil had disappeared.

'Krakik! Krakik!' Elya screamed. 'He's gone! Krakik! O somebody do something! Krakik! Krakik!' But the time for saving was past. Though animals and birds flocked to the cabin, and a search-party was quickly organised, no-one found any sign of the snake. Dreevil, using evil ways unknown to any of them, had escaped, and was far away by morning.

For some time, Elya's screams resounded in the forest. When Magis had receded, Elya splashed through the mud and, flinging herself at the foot of the tree, cried with hard, dry sobs that shook her body.

'I hate Dreevil!' she cried. 'I hate him!' And she beat the ground with the log of wood in her hand. 'He's wicked, wicked! O why didn't I go out of the cabin and try to save Krakik?'

Lauristal's waters stirred, and Trefoil held her gently in his strong roots. 'Elya', he said when she was quieter, 'Dreevil has frightened stronger people than you. You did your best. That is all that matters.'

'But I might have saved Krakik! If I'd only moved! I was too frightened!'

Trefoil looked at her gravely. 'This is a hard lesson, Elya, much harder than Rarebit imagined.'

Elya looked up with streaming eyes.

'You see, it was a matter of choice for Krakik . . . poor, old frog. It was not the first time they had dealings, you know. That was obvious. And dealings of any kind with Dreevil are dangerous.'

cabin tonight?' she pleaded. She was a pathetic figure in the early dawn.

Trefoil glanced at Rowlie, who tossed his mane and nodded his great head. Elya leant against him as they returned to the cabin.

'Do you think Krakik came here to get away from the snake, Trefoil?' Lauristal asked.

'I guess that was partly his purpose. The singing competition was the main attraction.'

'You don't suppose —?'

'Yes, I think Dreevil allowed him to come here, because he wanted to attack Elya through the frog.'

'Then why —?'

'It is hard to know Dreevil's mind, but my suspicion is that the frog was ready for destruction, and the temptation was too great for Dreevil to resist. He was sure of Krakik.'

'Then, Trefoil, that means —'

'— he will be back.'

'And there'll be danger for Elya?'

'There will be great danger for Elya.'

'Do you think she understands that?'

'Not at present, but it may dawn on her at any moment.'

Tricko darted from the forest to report to Trefoil. 'No sign of him anywhere', he said.

The tree nodded. 'That was to be expected. He is a wily old monster. Tricko, Elya has learnt quickly, but there is much still to learn. She must be guarded day and night for the present. Be careful not to frighten her. We want her to be prudent, however. She is not a forest creature who learns at birth how to act, but we can protect her until the time comes for her to be independent.'

'A roster?' Tricko asked. He moved his bushy tail.

'I thank the Master he has made you so reliable, Tricko.'

The fox bowed his head and glided into the forest.

CHAPTER FIVE

Tricko was gathering food for his family when he saw Elya slip out of the back door of her log cabin, run to the shelter of the forest, and creep through the bushes until she was opposite Trefoil.

The fox pounced.

'Oh!' Elya jumped. 'You frightened me, Tricko. Sh! I'm going to climb the tree.' She wriggled away from the fox's paws.

'Trefoil? Well . . .' Tricko was doubtful. 'Just you mind that you don't get into trouble. Can't imagine Trefoil enjoying a heavy lump like you in his branches.'

Elya chuckled. 'He's always telling me I'm too thin', she whispered and, leaving the fox, she tiptoed across the grass behind the tree.

When she was a short distance away, she ran and, leaping, caught hold of one of Trefoil's branches, swung herself on to a limb, scrambled over his boughs, and perched for a moment before climbing higher. Trefoil's roots jolted with surprise, but when he saw Elya, his trunk shook with laughter.

'So this is the way we have our lessons today', he rumbled and, catching her in his twigs, suspended her in the air above the pool.

Elya kicked and squealed. 'Trefoil! Trefoil! Let me go! . . . Please! Please!' she begged, as the tree rocked her back and forth like one of his own leaves. 'O Lauristal! Tell him to stop!'

'Cheek, cheek, cheek!' chirped Chirrik. 'You'll try to be a bird next, next, next!'

The tree suddenly dropped Elya on to one of his bigger branches, and the child remained there for the morning. She swung her legs; the sun shone in chequered patterns through the leaves; the swishing water sang in the distance.

From that time on, she sat in the tree for many of her lessons. Tricko made her a swing which hung from the strong branch across the pool, and, as summer approached, Elya played there. She would swing, drop in the pool to swim, climb once more into Trefoil's branches, and swing again.

One day, Haro came to the pool for a drink. 'Well, have you been prepared for the quest yet?' he asked.

Elya, sitting at the edge of the pool, her feet dangling in the water, looked up. 'What quest?' she asked.

'Trefoil, don't tell me you haven't mentioned the quest?' With lazy amusement, Haro turned to the tree. 'You must be failing!'

Trefoil was annoyed. 'You will remember, Haro, that at the forest assembly I was given the freedom to educate Elya in my own way.'

'Of course, of course, dear Trefoil.' Haro smiled. 'I thought that the quest would have been the first thing mentioned, that's all. It's the reason for the lessons, or so I imagined.'

'What's a quest?' asked Elya, puzzled.

Trefoil looked down on her upturned face. 'You will soon find out, Elya', said the tree. He was certainly not going to give a lesson on something so important while Haro was there to mock. 'Cheeky fellow!' he thought.

Haro raised his eyes to the sky and shrugged. Smiling a little, he bent his head to drink from the pool. Though Lauristal usually saved her sweetest water for the elders of the forest, she was often sorry that Haro's personality did not seem to grow any sweeter after drinking it.

'The quest, the quest', repeated Elya. 'It's a funny word. Lauristal, what's a quest?'

Lauristal glanced at Trefoil. 'There's no secret about it', she said, swishing her waters around Haro to show her displeasure. 'Everyone has a quest . . . but it's better if Trefoil tells you about it when you're ready.'

Just then, Rarebit, in search of Haro, came into the clearing.

'Rarebit!' exclaimed Elya. She forgot all about the interesting quest word, and ran toward the rabbit. Rarebit appeared embarrassed as she knelt to throw her arms about him and give him a hug.

'She's been missing the rabbit, it seems', mocked Haro.

'Where've you been?' asked Elya. Her eyes sparkled with excitement, and her face flushed. Rarebit came toward the pool, but he eyed Trefoil, and took care to keep out of the way of his strong branches.

'I've been workin' for Haro', he muttered, his chubby cheeks twitching with nervousness.

'Working!' Elya laughed. 'I thought you hated work, Rarebit.'

'My sort of work is like play.' Haro's expression, more than his words, told them that he thought Trefoil's teaching was too rigid. He bent to drink again.

Trefoil's branches shook with anger, but he kept silent. Even Lauristal, sweet-tempered as she usually was, swirled her waters until they looked dark in the sunlight.

'Good heavens, Lauristal, the living water tastes like bitter herbs these days!' Haro flicked one of the sparkling drops from his whiskers as he turned to go.

'But won't Rarebit stay?' pleaded Elya. 'I haven't seen him for ages.'

'Of course he can stay if he wants to. I'm certainly not stopping him.' He looked sternly at Rarebit, and the rabbit remained with Elya, while Haro loped gracefully away.

When Rarebit, urged by Haro, came every day to play with Elya, the swing was neglected. Elya understood why Rarebit was reluctant to play in Trefoil's branches. But, when Haro began to accompany Rarebit to the meadow each day, she found it hard to understand why they rarely went to drink Lauristal's living water.

Each morning, Elya woke to find Haro and Rarebit waiting outside the cabin, and she had breakfast with them. After lessons, they were waiting to lead her into the forest, where they played with her for hours till late at night. At any break during the day, they appeared, Haro in front, Rarebit trailing behind.

Elya thought Haro was wise, almost as wise as Trefoil, though not as ponderous. She spoke to the hare freely, and he listened solemnly. He watched while she romped with the rabbits. He told her stories by the hour. They were not the kind of story that Trefoil would like, Elya knew, but he was funny and she laughed and laughed. By degrees, she revealed more and more of the thoughts that came into her mind, and always Haro gave sound advice, at least to Elya's way of thinking, advice that was practical even if it was unkind at times.

If Trefoil was concerned, he did not show it. He had agreed with Lauristal that it was foolish to make a fuss without reason.

Magis never saw Elya these days. She was too busy to walk quietly along his banks and share life-thoughts with him. Haro and Rarebit had no love for Magis. They found him dull, and Elya, anxious to please, followed their leading.

Summer was a happy time for Elya. The long warm days with sunlight and shade, scented flowers and grasses, dense foliage and humming insects were a background for fun and laughter. Between Trefoil's lessons, which were so interesting that she liked them better than her play, her friends filled every second of her time.

On one of those few balmy evenings before autumn, Elya, with Rarebit and Haro, was sitting on the steps of the log cabin.

'Trefoil told me about the quest today', Elya said. Her eyes danced.

Haro looked down his nose. 'Oh? And what did the old fellow tell you?'

Elya disliked his expression, but she tried to ignore it. 'Everyone has the call to be', she said, 'but I don't understand that . . .'

'No wonder! I don't either. I wonder if Trefoil understands it himself.'

'O Haro, don't be so difficult!' exclaimed Elya. 'If Trefoil doesn't understand about quests, no-one does!'

'That's what I mean', said Haro, and said no more.

Elya, her forehead wrinkled in concentration, continued: 'It's a call . . . a call from the Master. Everyone has to follow it, and it's different for everyone. My call isn't the same as yours, and yours isn't Rarebit's.'

'Thank the skies for that', said Haro, raising his eyes.

Rarebit's ears reddened. He was often quiet these days.

Elya had not heard the hare because she was concentrating and trying to remember what Trefoil had taught her. 'There's something we're meant to be . . . as a person, I think Trefoil said, and we've got to find out what it is . . . It's like a journey to find a special treasure . . . I don't understand half of it, but Trefoil said I would, if I just took one step at a time.' She giggled. 'The trouble is, I don't know where to step to!'

'Sounds hard work to me', said Rarebit, yawning. 'I told you those lessons'd be hard an'dull . . . an' borin'.'

'Trefoil says that's part of the quest, Rarebit. He says there's always pain if you want something with all your heart.'

'And do you want to go on the quest?' asked Haro, his hard bright eyes searching her face.

Elya was absorbed in her thoughts. 'I think so. It sounds exciting. I don't know whether I can wait, though. I hate waiting, and Trefoil says you have to wait for the call. O dear! It's all so difficult.'

'Personally, I think you can live without that kind of quest', said Haro. 'Life's much easier . . . but don't tell Trefoil I said so.'

Elya looked at him doubtfully. 'What do you mean, Haro?'

Haro buttoned his mouth and wriggled his nose. After some minutes he said: 'You'll find out. I'm doing a bit of research at the moment, but I doubt if Trefoil or Lauristal would approve.' He stood still for a minute, and wiggled his ears. Suddenly his voice lashed out. 'Trefoil! He thinks he knows everything. I'll show him!'

Elya was startled by his bitterness.

'Lauristal and Trefoil and Magis! The three of them! You'd think there was no other wisdom in the world!' Haro turned and hopped away, and of course Rarebit, big blue eyes wide with surprise, followed him.

After that, Haro only occasionally came to the clearing. He usually sent Rarebit instead.

'Is Haro jealous of Trefoil?' asked Elya one day.

Rarebit jumped. 'Course not. He doesn't need to be jealous. He's the greatest! Anyway, there are lots of ways of doin' things.'

'What things?' asked Elya, but the rabbit looked at her vaguely, and changed the subject.

So the days went on, and, since Elya saw Rarebit more often than Haro, she talked to the rabbit about her lessons, ideas, and thoughts. Sometimes she thought about the hare and the rabbit. 'I respect Haro, and I admire his strength and wisdom . . . but Rarebit . . . I've always loved Rarebit!'

Lauristal often said to the tree: 'Elya thinks the world of that rabbit! Nothing good can come of it, Trefoil.'

It was not as though they could find fault with him. He was a pleasant little fellow, who never appeared to say anything wrong. In fact, he was silent when Trefoil was listening. He was anxious to please, too anxious, but there was nothing wrong with that. Lauristal was unable to say why she was worried. Magis guessed, but he would speak only when it was proved one way or the other. He sent his waters roaring to the sea, sad that he had lost the child, but glad that at least Trefoil and Lauristal still had a hold on her.

Elya noticed, one day, that some of the vegetables and tirips leaves in her cabin had disappeared. She was puzzled. Food never disappeared. It was a gift from her friends, and the cabin was open all day.

'Did anyone go to the cabin when I was having lessons?' she asked Chirrik.

Chirrik chirped briskly: 'Well, of course, if you make friends with silly creatures like that rabbit, rabbit, rabbit, what can you expect, expect, expect?'

'Rarebit? But Rarebit would've asked me. He knows he can always share with me!' cried Elya.

'He went to the cabin today, today, today', said Chirrik. 'Saw him myself, self, self. Creeping in like a guilty thief. Silly rabbit, rabbit, rabbit!' she scoffed, and flew off.

'Well, what does it matter?' thought Elya. Yet the idea worried her. 'He could've asked me. He knew I'd never refuse.'

When Rarebit called for her again, she confronted him. 'Rarebit', she said, 'some of the vegetables in my cabin were missing yesterday. Do you know anything about them?'

Rarebit twitched his nose several times before answering. His round, rabbit face flushed, but he opened his big eyes wide to show his innocence. 'What vegetables?' he asked.

Elya knew from his expression that he was the culprit. 'Carrots and lettuce and tirips leaves. They disappeared', she said crisply.

Rarebit wriggled. 'I don't know anythin' about any carrots', he said. 'Elya, are you accusin' me? That's how much you trust your friends!' Angrily he turned and hopped down the pathway. Elya thought he was relieved to escape, because he avoided the tree, only pausing to glance over his shoulder at Trefoil.

The tree's hearing was acute, his observation sharp. At once he saw that Elya was upset. 'Elya', he called. 'What is the matter?'

Elya sat at the side of the pool, and poured out her tale. 'I trusted him', she said. 'I can't believe he would treat me like that. I didn't have the chance to say he could take vegetables whenever he wanted them. It's not that. It's the sneakiness that matters!'

'He will come round', said the tree patting her on the head. 'He will soon forget. And he will expect you to forget, too.'

Trefoil was right. Rarebit did come back. He said nothing about the missing food, and Elya, delighted to see him, did her best to forget the whole incident.

In the meantime, she had time to think, and she realised that she was neglecting Magis. She returned to her custom of walking along his banks and listening to his rumbles, and she learnt more from silent communication with him than from all Trefoil's lessons.

As winter approached, she invited Rarebit to sit in the cabin and share the warmth of her fire and her meal. They chatted and laughed and played games to while away the long autumn evenings. Later, Rowlie or Tricko or one of the tigers would arrive on guard as they had done since Krakik's disappearance, and Rarebit would reluctantly hop into the chilly night to find his burrow. Elya slept soundly these nights.

The annual holidays always came in winter. Elya had instructions to work in her garden, though most of it would be under snow before long. Otherwise she would be free to run and walk in the forest, and play. 'There will be no danger from Dreevil', said Trefoil, 'because he has probably gone underground like other snakes'.

In Living Water Country, unlike other lands, Magis never allowed his water to freeze in winter. It was too important for the well-being of the inhabitants. Though birds and animals kept to their homes during the day, in the evening all the forest creatures came to drink at the pool. Lauristal sparkled whether the skies glowered or the sun smiled, whether the land slept in snowy silence or leapt to life with glittering crystals.

'I'll see you in spring', said Rarebit one day. 'I'm goin' away on holidays tomorrer.'

'O, where are you going?' Elya was surprised and disappointed at the same time. This was the first she had heard of holidays.

'Somewhere near Saltbush Plains. Haro's goin' on business, and he's takin' me with him.' Rarebit stroked his bobtail importantly.

'But what about the living water?' asked Elya. 'You'll need some, won't you?'

'For gosh sakes, Elya! You're a baby!' Rarebit was contemptuous. 'There'll be plenty of snow around. Who needs water?'

'It's special', said Elya.' It makes you want to live forever!'

'Well, I'm alive, aren't I?' said Rarebit, and he hopped away.

'Is Haro coming to see me before he goes?' Elya called after him.

The rabbit turned, and gave her a cheeky grin. 'Nah! Too busy, he says!' He disappeared into the forest, and left Elya cut off from his friendship 'like a branch of a tree sliced from its trunk', as she told Trefoil later.

The tree nodded sadly.

CHAPTER SIX

When the idea first came to Tricko, he was very pleased with himself. In his wisdom he realised that Elya would miss the rabbit, and would be lonely during the long winter holidays, and he had been trying to think what he could do about it. Now he knew. His bushy tail waved as he ran into the forest.

His first job was to beg wood and gum from the trees. The trees knew the clever fox. He had often helped them, so they gave gladly.

He then persuaded Chirrik to ask the other birds for feathers, a difficult task because, as the winter grew colder, anything warm was precious. However, Chirrik had been Tricko's friend for a long time, and once she made up her mind about something, it would have been an extraordinary bird that could have refused her. The birds gathered a large heap of feathers and put them near the fox's lair.

Finally, Tricko went to a well-known bee's hive. He charmed the sleepy bees into giving him some of their wax.

When Tricko had gathered all his materials, including a bundle of reeds, he began, with his sharp teeth, to carve the wood. Lovingly he shaped and polished until the mellow, red wood was formed, at last, into a neat little sled. It took him days to clean his tail which was coated with beeswax, but he was so pleased with his work that he thought it was worth the trouble.

When the structure was finished, he carefully panelled the sled with soft feathers, gummed them together, and padded the seat with dried grass.

One day, after a fall of snow, Tricko and his sled arrived at Elya's cabin. At the sound of his knock, Elya woke and stretched.

Tricko opened the door and called: 'Here's something you'll like'. His sharp, green eyes darted a look of amusement at Rowlie, who was sleepily rubbing his big face and yawning, as he rolled over on the wooden floor.

Elya jumped out of bed and ran to the door. 'Oh!' she gasped.

Rowlie opened one eye, and caught sight of Tricko's handiwork. 'A sled!' he exclaimed, opening both eyes. He pulled himself up, and padded to the door to look over Elya's shoulder. 'Why, bless me! You clever old fox!'

'It's beautiful, Tricko', said Elya. She ran down the steps, and walked round the sled. The polished wood winked at her in the weak rays of the sun.

'Like a ride?' asked Tricko smiling. 'Not you, Rowlie. You're too big!'

The lion pretended to be disappointed. 'Gone are the days —'

'You'd make a wonderful horse.' Elya was jigging with excitement.

While Elya went inside to fling on some warm clothes, Tricko harnessed the good-natured lion in the plaited reed ropes.

A minute later, Elya ran down the steps and settled herself on the sled. She flicked an imaginary whip, and the lion drew her smoothly across the blanket of snow covering her garden. Only the tops of bushes peeped at them through the white wilderness. Rowlie padded heavily, and took pleasure in making the snow squeak underfoot. The sled hissed softly behind him.

Elya made the two animals pause now and then to look at the icicles that had dropped from her fruit trees. Tufts of snow, caught in the leafless branches, had melted, dripped, and frozen again before they reached the ground. They glistened like crystal.

The air was crisp and cold. Tricko, eyes watchful, enjoyed the slow journey as much as Elya and Rowlie. The forest, however, was Tricko's element, and as they entered together, his muscles tingled. He looked at the wondering face of the child, who was breathing deeply.

Evergreen trees, laden with snow, and trunks encrusted with a million tiny jewels, opened white crystal arms to welcome them, while smaller trees bowed to the earth. A sea of snowy softness surrounded them in a hushed, white world.

Elya, silent, her face alive, gazed around her. Snow-clad trees crisped a greeting.

'Thank you', Elya piped. She scarcely recognised her own voice.

'Lucky young thing to have holidays!' growled Rowlie, freeing himself from the ropes. 'Well, I must be off and about my business. I'll see you later, Tricko.' He strode off, swinging his tail behind him.

Elya jumped out of the sled. Frosty powder showered her. She brushed it away with a gloved hand, paused, and bent over to roll a snowball. Straightening suddenly, she threw it at the fox. The snow caught Tricko on his face. He recovered from the surprise, and jumped behind a tree. From that moment, he kept up such a continuous cannon of snowballs that Elya, panting and laughing, had to plead for mercy.

'Come now', said Tricko, shaking the snow from his back. 'I'll show you how to use the sled.'

Elya followed him through the trees to the slopes he had found for her. 'Once you've learnt how to manage it, you'll never be without company', Tricko said. Taking the plaited reed ropes, he began to pull the sled.

Elya danced up to the fox, and gave him a hug. Her kiss caught him on the end of his nose.

'Herru-u-mph!' Tricko looked shy, but he was pleased too. He took her where the snow slides were particularly good, and showed her how to direct the sled down the hill and walk up again.

During the next weeks, Elya had no time to miss Rarebit, because many of the smaller animals of the forest asked her for rides, and she was kept busy running up and down the slopes all day long, or drawing the sled across the flat areas, where the freshness of crackling snow, the cold dry air, and the snow-swept slopes around her soaked into her being. Exercise helped her body grow healthy and supple. Her cheeks glowed.

Trefoil and Lauristal were delighted to see her so happy, and were grateful to the fox.

On one of these occasions she met, half-hidden behind a rock, a small shivering mouse who timidly watched her.

Elya stopped. 'Would you like a ride?' she asked, smiling. The warm feather cap that Chirrik had given her had slipped over one eye, and she pushed it back on her head to see the mouse more clearly.

He was round, fat, and very furry, but his little nose twitched in terror. 'Come on', said Elya kindly. 'I won't hurt you. It's fun.'

The mouse hunched his back. 'I might stop your fun', he squeaked. 'I'm not very good at things like this.'

'You don't have to be good at sledding to enjoy it', Elya said. 'Hop on, and I'll take you up the hill.'

The mouse stumbled on to the sled, rolled over, and, struggled upright. 'S-s-sorry!' he said. 'I'm so awkward!

Elya laughed. 'O don't be silly.' She began to mount the white slope, which was marked and ruffled by her many journeys.

'Yes, I am silly', said the mouse. 'Everyone thinks so. I can't help it.'

Elya looked at him in surprise. 'What's your name?' she asked.

'It's not a nice name, I'm afraid', apologised the mouse. 'It's . . . er . . . Poorme!'

Elya's eyes twinkled, and she was about to tease him, when she noticed his black eyes blinking miserably. She felt sorry for him. Just in time, she choked back her joke.

Suddenly the mouse slid from one side of the sled to the other. 'Goodness! Don't fall off. Grip the side!' said Elya.

'Sorry!' gasped Poorme, red to his ears. 'I'm always doing something wrong!' He grasped the feather lining, while Elya, without another word in case she embarrassed him further, plodded to the top of the slope.

She heard Chirrik singing in the distance, and sang her own song as she moved.

'In the forest, through the glades
Master craftsman lingers, weaves
white carpet, silver trees,
shining snowflakes, crystal leaves.'

'I haven't got much of a singing voice', squeaked the mouse, cringing in the corner of the sled.

Elya stopped singing. 'It doesn't matter', she said consolingly.

'I'm not much good at anything, I'm afraid', groaned the mouse.

Elya began to feel cross. She pursed her lips and said nothing until they reached the top of the hill.

'Now, move up, Poorme', she said. 'I'll guide the sled, and you hang on.'

'I hope I won't be a nuisance.'

'Of course you won't be a nuisance', said Elya tartly. 'I invited you, didn't I?'

'Sorry!' muttered the mouse.

Elya was busy guiding the sled. For once, the slide was bumpy. The sled jerked, and Elya had to use all her skill to move it in a smooth path down the hill. Poorme bumped in front of her, and nearly lost his balance.

'O sorry!' he gasped again, and Elya put out a hand to steady him, lost control, and they both went tumbling in the snow.

Normally, Elya would have thought this hilarious. It had happened before, and she had found more enjoyment with her friends than if the ride had gone according to plan. This time, however, the mouse was causing her real annoyance. 'Now, see what you've done!' she snapped.

Poorme cowered in the snow. 'I'm so sorry', he said, 'so very sorry . . . I'm always being a nuisance to everyone. I just seem to cause trouble wherever I go. I'm so sorry!'

'If you say you're sorry once again, I'll scream!' said Elya.

'I make everyone scream', said Poorme miserably. 'I do apologise.'

'Oh-h-h you!' exclaimed Elya. She stamped her foot. 'Anyway, you're still sitting there looking miserable. Are you hurt or not?'

Poorme stood awkwardly on his two hind feet, and stretched himself. 'No-o-o. I don't think so. Why do I always cause accidents wherever I go? No, a few bruises, I think.' He swayed a little.

Elya sighed. 'You'd better come to Lauristal', she said. 'She'll know what to do.'

'O I couldn't!' said the mouse. 'O I really couldn't intrude on anyone, especially the great Lauristal.'

'But surely you go there for the living water. All the other animals do!'

'O I'm really not good enough', said Poorme, desperate with anxiety. 'Of no account at all. Not like other animals.'

'Well, you're going this time', said Elya, and, placing Poorme inside her coat to keep him warm, she trudged back to the cabin. The gleaming sled moved smoothly behind her. The mouse trembled violently. 'Poor little thing', she thought, 'but he's annoying, too, with all this "sorry" business'.

She left the sled at the cabin door, and marched across the clearing to Trefoil. The sun, which had been hidden all the afternoon, streamed through the grey clouds at the same moment, and lit up the white, laden tree mirrored in the shining pool.

Elya carefully took out the mouse and put him on the ground beside Lauristal. 'This is Poorme', she announced. 'He says he's never had living water.'

The poor little creature shivered and bowed himself close to the ground. 'I'm so sorry!' he murmured.

'Well, so you should be', said the tree mildly. 'Surely you know that the living water is important for growth. What kept you away so long?'

The mouse looked at him timidly. 'I didn't think I was good enough', he said.

'How silly!' scolded Elya. 'No-one is good enough. That's not the point, is it Trefoil? The living water is there to help us, isn't it?'

'Indeed', nodded the tree, and smiled at her. 'You have learnt some lessons well, Elya.'

'I don't think I dare drink it', whimpered Poorme. 'I'm so stupid, and I'll never be able to live up to it. Never! Isn't it better to go without, than to take it when you're unworthy?'

Lauristal's laugh tinkled. 'O you poor, little thing', she said. 'Where did you learn such nonsense? No-one is worthy, least of all myself who carry it for others.'

'O dear! What a mess I make of everything!' moaned the mouse.

'Poorme', reflected Trefoil. 'Yes, I see why you are called that. It is a nickname, I suppose?'

'I had another name, but I don't remember it now. Everyone calls me Poorme, because I am, you know.'

'O do stop that!' exclaimed Elya. 'You're a pretty, little mouse, isn't he, Lauristal? You've got soft fur, and it shines like Trefoil's leaves in summer. And you've got such nice pink ears . . .'

'And charming brown eyes', added the pool.

Poorme shuffled his tiny feet, and his ears reddened. Elya giggled.

'You're making fun of me!' Poorme whimpered.

Lauristal looked compassionately at the small embarrassed creature, and Elya stopped laughing. 'Do believe me when I say we're your friends', said Lauristal earnestly. 'We're not laughing at you, but with you. You need to laugh at yourself!'

'That's easy!' Poorme was bitter.

'No, it's not easy for you, Poorme', said Lauristal. 'Your laughter mocks. Why do you think so little of yourself?'

'Because I'm no good', said Poorme, and his dark eyes filled with tears. 'I've never been any good for myself or anyone really, though I try so hard all the time.'

'You try too hard', said Lauristal. 'Stop blaming yourself.'

'I'm sorry!' said the mouse.

'If you didn't take yourself so seriously . . . Look . . . it's important to be gentle with yourself, as well as others.'

'I don't seem to be able to get on with others', said Poorme. 'I'm always trying, but I always do the wrong thing. I'm sorry, but that's the way it is.' He lowered his head on his paws, and hid his face.

'It's a job for Magis', said Lauristal, looking inquiringly at the tree, who nodded.

'Elya, go and walk with Poorme along Magis's banks', she said, 'and if Poorme can't find anything to say, I'm sure you can. You chatter to him long enough.'

Poorme's eyes had grown so wide with fright that they almost covered his tiny face. 'Me? Talk to Magis? O . . . but what would I talk about? I wouldn't know what to say. O I couldn't!'

'Don't be silly!' said Elya, with childish practicality. 'I do talk to him sometimes, but I listen mostly. He tells me things.'

Trefoil looked pleased.

'Magis will tell you what to do, Poorme', encouraged Lauristal gently. 'Just go with Elya, and when you come back, I'll have some of my best water for you . . . Poor little mouse!' she added, as Elya, with the mouse in her hand, moved out of sight.

An hour passed, and another. There was no sign of Elya and the mouse. The tree was about to send the breeze messenger in search of the pair, when they rounded the corner.

Elya's face was alight with an inner peace, and the mouse looked dazed as she placed him again at the side of the pool. 'He knows what to do', Elya said to the tree, 'but I'm not sure if he'll do it'.

Poorme stayed at the side of the pool for many days after that. He was always timid and shy, and was always apologising. Trefoil and Lauristal left him to himself. They made sure Elya did not interfere with him either.

Chirrik, however, had her own way of doing things. 'You! Poorme!' she chirped, one day. Poorme jumped. 'You'll be getting so fat that you won't be able to move if you sit there all the time, time, time!' she said briskly.

Poorme blushed to the tips of his soft little ears. 'Well . . . er . . . yes . . . I have put on a little weight lately. I must do something about it, I suppose', he apologised.

'You certainly should, should, should!' said Chirrik. 'A fat fool isn't in it, in it, in it!' She flew to a nearby tree.

Poorme was flabbergasted. The attack was so sudden. He looked at his waistline, and patted his plump little legs. 'I didn't think I was as bad as that!' he said.

Elya grinned, and Trefoil tapped her sharply on the head.

'O dear, I must look terrible!' said Poorme. He tried to hide himself under a stone.

Chirrik swooped again, and tweaked him by the tail. 'Fatty! Fatty! Fatty!' she chirped.

The mouse burst into tears. 'I can't help it', he said. 'It's not my fault. I'll never be any good for anything.'

Chirrik sat on Trefoil's branch stretching across the pool. 'Cowardy, cowardy, custard, custard, custard!' she chirped.

'O I'm sorry!' gasped the mouse. 'O this is terrible! I wish I'd never been born!'

Elya, surprised that Trefoil and Lauristal let the bird behave like this, started forward to rescue him. Trefoil held her back.

Once again Chirrik swooped. 'Into the pool you go, you fat little fool, fool, fool!' With her beak, she tumbled him into the deepest part of the pool's cold waters.

Elya watched Poorme sink. 'Trefoil!' she cried. 'It's cold. He'll drown! Let me go! I must help him!'

'He will be safe. Leave him', commanded Trefoil. 'Just watch.'

With a roar, Magis's waters burst into the pool. The mouse struggled, but the waters closed around him, and he was whirled in a spiral, round and round and round. Poor Poorme! He was tossed like a cork, now this way, now that. Desperately, he put out his paws, and clung with all his strength to the rocks at the side of the pool. The waters battered him to and fro, and fro and to, until he was dizzy and bruised.

Elya looked on in amazement as the tiny mouse was thrown to the top of the pool. Something had happened to Poorme. He was red with anger. 'I refuse to be broken', he said loudly.

Lauristal's waters, suddenly calm, seemed to listen.

Poorme disappeared, and then, gasping, he appeared above water again. 'I want to live!' he shouted.

Lauristal's waters cleared.

Poorme's head disappeared for a second time, and for a second time rose again. 'I won't drown!' he yelled. 'I'm going to live and use my gifts!' He struggled to the side of the pool.

The sun shone with dazzling brightness.

'Chirrik, pull me out!' screamed Poorme.

Chirrik, chuckling, took the little fellow in her beak, and dropped him at the side of the pool. 'I'm sorry, sorry, sorry!' she warbled.

Poorme began to smile. His smile widened to become a chuckle. The chuckle became a throaty laugh, and then he giggled and giggled and giggled, and rolled over and over on the grass beside the pool, until Elya thought he must be ill. Trefoil and Lauristal laughed in sympathy.

'How foolish I've been!' said Poorme sitting up at last. 'Always apologising. But I'm going to forget all that.' He wiped his streaming eyes. 'Anyway, I'm not so foolish that I'm staying a poor me. I'm going to be a true me in future. I've just remembered, that's my name. Trueme!' He laughed.

At last, he jumped up. 'I've taken too much of your time', he said, 'but I've learnt a big lesson. If I think of myself as a poor me, I'll be one, and if I think of myself as a true me, then I'll be that, too. It's simple, really!'

'You have learnt more than one lesson', said Trefoil solemnly. 'The power of Magis, the need for the living water, to say nothing of a healthy love of yourself.'

'Thank you all so much', said Trueme, 'especially you, you wicked bird!' he called to Chirrik.

'I'll be back to ride on your sled, Elya', he squeaked, as he ran off.

Before reaching the edge of the clearing, he called to Lauristal. 'I'm coming every night for the living water. Try to keep me away.'

As Trueme turned toward the forest, he knocked into a clump of frozen fern. 'O I'm so sorry', he said, but he stopped and grinned at himself. Then, drawing himself to his full mouse's height, he bowed politely. 'Perhaps you would grow somewhere else in future.'

And, chuckling at his own impertinence, Trueme scampered into the forest.

CHAPTER SEVEN

As Elya ran into the meadow one day in early spring, two heads appeared above the grass at the edge of the forest.

'Haro! Rarebit!' Elya ran excitedly toward them.

'Elya, you've grown!' Haro hopped back to look at her. She had. In her eleventh year, Elya was as slim as she had been as a small child, but now she seemed to be made up of tanned legs and arms. During the winter months, her hair had grown longer. Straight, and soft, it flowed over her shoulders in shining ripples, rivalling Lauristal's waters. Her dark eyes glowed.

Rarebit was rounder and fatter than she remembered, which suggested that he had eaten well during his holiday in the west. Otherwise, he had not changed much. His eyes were still round and blue, but they had lost their sparkle.

But the hare! Something had changed Haro. He had the same brown and white fur, and was still dignified and aloof, but Elya, gazing at him, felt a chill round her heart. His features were hard, his expression mocking.

'Well, and do you know all about the quest, now?' the hare asked at last.

The quest? Elya had not thought of the quest lately. Trefoil said she would know when the time came, and she was happy to wait, but she did not know how to say this to Haro, so she simply smiled at him.

'Well, actually', said the hare, 'I'm on a quest myself at the moment'. He looked at her intently, waiting for her response.

'That should be very nice for you, Haro', Elya said politely.

'Yes', said the hare, 'I'm going to the Great Mountains to find my destiny'.

'You're going away? But you've just come back!'

The hare preened himself. 'One must follow the call', he said.

'Of course', said Elya doubtfully. There was something wrong about this, but she was not quite sure what it was. She had an idea. 'O do come and tell Trefoil and Lauristal. They'll be so interested.'

Haro hesitated, but the temptation to show his importance to the tree was too much. 'Very well', he agreed. Rarebit wrinkled his nose in distaste, but he followed Haro closely. They walked through Elya's garden, where bulbs were pushing through the damp earth and the bushes and trees were showing the first fuzz of soft green leaves. The tree was washed in sunlight as they approached.

'Haro and Rarebit are back!' cried Elya, flinging herself at the side of the pool. 'And Haro has news, Trefoil.'

The tree politely rustled his leaves. Lauristal smiled a welcome. It was a long time since they had visited her, and she thought: 'What a pity it is that they do not drink the living water nowadays!'

'I'm off on the quest, Trefoil', said Haro, 'off to the mountains to see what I can find to add to my store of knowledge'.

Trefoil frowned. 'The quest?' he asked, and then added: 'A strange quest, Haro, as you well know!'

'I know nothing of the sort', Haro said. 'Knowledge is surely a quest worth following.'

Elya was bewildered. 'Why is Trefoil not smiling?' she wondered.

'Knowledge, wisdom, and understanding go together', Trefoil reminded the hare. 'True knowledge is only found in humble ways.'

'Stuff and nonsense!' cried Haro. 'No-one believes that these days. You must be getting old!'

Lauristal was still. 'Magis's waters are ever new', she said gently. 'Haro, you must drink before you go . . . to give you strength.'

'I'm strong enough', said Haro impatiently. 'I don't need your waters, Lauristal. Never again! I'm tired of crystal waters and such. What good does it do? Now, tell me . . .'

Elya could scarcely believe she was hearing aright. 'Haro!' she exclaimed.

'Elya, you're growing into a bore, young as you are', interrupted Haro. 'Too much time with these three-in-one creatures! Magis has influenced Lauristal and Trefoil for years, and now you're being infected — yes, in-fected, I said. You'll blow up one of these days.'

Elya gaped at him. 'Close your mouth, child', Haro snapped. 'I'm following my own quest in my own way, so it's no use arguing.'

'So, that is the problem!' murmured Trefoil.

'No problem, Trefoil. What fools you all are to wait round for a quest! It's much easier to find your own!' Haro hopped up and down in his excitement, and knocked Rarebit backwards. The rabbit tumbled over and over, and sat up flustered and hurt. Elya put her arm around him, but Rarebit fixed his eyes on Haro, and remained motionless.

'So', continued Haro, 'like it or not, Trefoil, I'm finding my way to the mountains through the swamp'. He stood on his back legs, and faced Trefoil defiantly.

'You are being foolish!' warned Trefoil.

'Foolish, eh? Well, we'll see about that. Commonsense should tell you that it's the easiest way. Go by Magis, and see the difficulty of rough ways. I'm telling you, the swamp has water . . . a little muddy, no doubt, but mud can be relaxing to hares, you know . . . wide open spaces . . . without trees.' He looked sharply at Trefoil, who did not respond. 'Plenty of grass', he said, waving his paws. 'Fine earth for burrows . . .'

'Who told you this?' asked Trefoil.

'A friend', said Haro airily. 'And I've been as far as Saltbush Plains for a visit, so I've seen it. Anyway, how will you go to the Great Mountains yourself, when the time comes . . . rooted, old tree?' Haro wrinkled his nose in contempt.

Elya flushed. 'Haro, you shouldn't talk to Trefoil like that!' she exclaimed.

'You shouldn't talk to Trefoil like that!' the hare mimicked.

'O Haro, don't be so mean! We had such lovely times together last summer.' Elya was almost in tears. 'Wouldn't you like to stay for a while?'

'No, Elya, I must go while the weather's fine. But you could always come with me', said Haro, smiling wickedly at the tree.

'But the swamp! Full of snakes and crocodiles! What about Dreevil?' Elya wailed.

'Leave Dreevil to me', said Haro. 'I know how to handle him. In any case, there are worse things here than Dreevil.' He watched Trefoil with narrowed eyes.

'Haro, I appeal to you, for the sake of your friends, if you must go to the Great Mountains without a call, at least go by way of Magis', Trefoil said, pain in every leaf as he looked at the rebellious hare.

Haro wiggled his ears. 'You interfering old trunk', he said at last. 'Mind your own business!' He took Elya's hand. 'Goodbye, Elya. If you'd like to come with me, contact me in the next few days. Otherwise, it'll be too late.'

Elya leant over to stroke the rabbit. Her tears soaked his fur and scalded his skin. Rarebit moved restlessly.

'Haro, Haro!' called the tree as the hare loped away, but there was no answer. Haro cared nothing for the gentle laws of the forest. He was going his own way on a new adventure, and he was sure he was right.

Elya talked to the rabbit as they walked across the clearing.

'Yes, it's a loss', Rarebit agreed, when Elya shared her grief. 'Yes, it's a risk', he nodded. But as Elya talked more and more earnestly, he suddenly shook his bobtail and said, yawning: 'P'rhaps it's better to take risks. He won't get dull that way.'

Elya was confused, but she surprised herself by saying: 'There are risks that give life, and others that bring death, Rarebit. I hope Haro knows that.'

'Course he does', said Rarebit coldly. 'What're you makin' a fuss for?'

Elya blushed. 'Do I really know these two animals?' she wondered. 'I have often shared my thoughts with them . . . but they have never shared with me', she realised suddenly.

'You know I love Haro', she said to the rabbit.

Rarebit shook his ears impatiently, and before long he departed, leaving Elya alone.

She waited for Rarebit the next day, and the next, but there was no sign of him. Trefoil watched her wait anxiously till the sun went down, and her face grew pale and drawn. Shoulders drooping, she went to the cabin.

A few days later Chirrik brought the news. 'Tidings of that silly rabbit, rabbit, rabbit!' she chirped. 'He's gone with Haro, Haro, Haro.'

'Oh-h-h-h!' The wail was from Elya, who had come to the pool for a drink. 'O silly, silly rabbit!' she cried. 'And he didn't even say goodbye or anything. He must have been thinking of it all along. O Trefoil!'

Trefoil stretched his old branches over the child. He felt old, and sick, and worn. Haro was right in calling him an old dead trunk, he thought. He was feeling that way these days, but he must do his best.

'Elya', he said, clearing his throat, 'the problem is not yours. It is Haro's and Rarebit's. Why make it your own?'

'They're my friends', wailed Elya.

A cold shudder of fear flowed down Trefoil's branches.

The child's tears dried as she sat with her face hidden against the tree. She was quiet for a time, so still that Trefoil thought his heart would stop beating with the fear that gripped him. He dared not speak. Elya, this time, would make her decision without him, and he would do nothing to sway her. He must not. He had led her to this point, the point of choice.

'I'll have to go after them, Trefoil, you know that. I can't sit back and let them go into danger . . . not after Krakik!' Elya's voice, clear and firm, tingled among his leaves.

The tree became grey in the evening light, and Lauristal held her waters.

'It'll be safer with three', Elya said eagerly. 'Dreevil will hardly attack the three of us. Trefoil . . . Lauristal . . .? O I know you don't like it, but I must try, somehow, to bring them back.'

She jumped up, and ran to the cabin.

'At least take some living water with you', called Lauristal, her voice breaking. Elya went into the cabin, and reappeared with a strong leather bottle her father had used. She quickly filled it with water. 'I have to hurry, Lauristal. Say goodbye to Magis for me . . . and Trefoil, don't look so sad. I'll be back, you'll see.' Flinging her arms about his trunk, she gave him a quick hug, and then ran to the cabin to gather food in a grass blanket. She threw it over her shoulder as she left.

Rowlie and Tricko were waiting for her. 'You're making a mistake, Elya', growled Rowlie. 'The way of Magis is the way to the Great Mountains.'

Tricko signed to him to silence. Elya tried to keep her voice steady. 'I know that, Rowlie. If it was just me, I would never try to go by way of the swamp. Trefoil knows that. But I must do everything I can to bring Haro and Rarebit back, and if I can't persuade them, I can at least try to help them on the journey. Trefoil has given me lots of lessons to guard me against Dreevil . . . and with three against one . . .'

'Never trust Dreevil', said Tricko quickly. 'He has piled up cunning over the centuries. Are you taking some living water?'

Elya nodded. 'In that is your greatest hope.' Tricko's face, however, showed his anxiety, but he said no more.

'We'll come with you as far as Saltbush Plains', growled Rowlie. 'We can't go any further.'

'I'm worried about Haro and Rarebit', Elya said. 'O, do understand, Rowlie. It's not because I don't care for all my other friends, but I can't help remembering what happened to Krakik, and I must try to help them.'

The two animals bowed their heads. They could not agree with her, but she had her own reasons, and must make her own decision. Elya waved to Lauristal, Trefoil, and the great river. Accompanied by her friends, she moved with determined steps through the clearing and into the forest.

Later, as they watched Elya fading into the distance on Saltbush Plains, Tricko murmured to Rowlie: 'We can only hope she can find her way through the shadows of darkness'.

The lion tossed his mane. 'May the Master's wind and stars protect her', he said.

'Amen to that.'

The two animals turned back to their forest homes.

CHAPTER EIGHT

Elya, feeling very lonely without Tricko and Rowlie, took the path they had shown her, and moved across the ugly wasteland. There were muddy pools everywhere, and stiff yellow sword-grass so different from the soft green carpet in Living Water Country.

'I won't be able to sit there', Elya thought. The grass shivered in the wind.

Travelling was easy in this flat, bare land. A road, covered in fine dry grit set like concrete, was as smooth and straight as Haro had said. There were no bumps, no pebbles, no potholes. In the distance, in the direction of the river, barren ragged rocks rose in great outcrops, and a few saltbushes grew in scattered clumps across the plain. Otherwise, the scenery was incredibly boring.

'No wonder it's called Saltbush Plains', Elya thought. 'There's nothing else!'

The sun, an angry yellow, was high in the sky when she sat at the side of the road. She unpacked the food she had brought with her, and began eating. Some of the fruit was already overripe, so reluctantly she had to throw it away, but she ate two juicy apples and felt refreshed. The sun shone relentlessly, the air was damp. There was no sound, not even the chirp of birds or the buzz of insects.

'I wonder if it's always dreary like this', Elya said to herself. 'Krakik must have made enough noise when he lived here.' The memory of the frog saddened her, and made her even more determined to do what she could for Haro and Rarebit. 'I wish everything wasn't so weird!' she said aloud. Her heart thumped as her voice echoed in the strange silence. She must be the only living thing in all this part of the world!

Shivering in spite of the heat, Elya once more carefully packed her blanket and continued her long march across the plains.

Hours went by, and still she walked wearily onwards. The sun began to sink beyond the distant hills, and Elya's heart sank with it. In the daytime she could be brave; in the night she was always timid, especially after Dreevil's attack on Krakik. This strange land was enough to frighten the bravest heart.

By this time, Elya felt so tired she simply had to rest. She hated the thought of spending the night in the open. Tears were close as she looked around for a tree or a bush to give her shelter.

'Elya, Elya!' The squeaky voice behind her made her jump. Along the path, up her leg, and into the palm of her hand, raced a little, round furry creature.

'Trueme!' cried Elya, all her weariness forgotten. 'O you dear little pet!'

'I've come to keep you company. I heard from Chirrik that you were coming. I have some cousins living not far from here, and I've visited them sometimes. I don't like the place, but I do know the surroundings a little.' Trueme was no longer the timid Poorme thinking of himself all the time, but a smiling, confident, little creature, his soft grey fur glowing in the strange sun.

'Thank you, Trueme.' Elya gently stroked his fur with her finger.

'Are you too tired to go on?' asked the mouse. 'This isn't the best place to stop, you know. No-one lives here, because it's too open. Dreevil'd see us easily if he's about. If you can manage another short distance, you'll be at the end of the plains near the swamp. I know a place where we could sleep safely for the night.' The tiny creature jumped on her shoulder, and began to sing in his squeaky little voice:

'Taradil, taradil, onward we go,
walking and marching and pointing the toe,
dancing and prancing right over the plains,

singing and ringing, our voices we raise,

Taradil, taradil, all of our days'.

Elya, who thought she had not an ounce of energy left, found herself walking in time to the merry tune. She laughed, and Trueme's little voice rang in the silence.

And then, just when she really felt she could go no further, but must drop to the ground, she saw in the distance the glimmer of a fire with two shadowy figures bending over it.

'Look!' she cried, and Trueme said: 'By all that's wonderful! They must be your friends!'

Elya tried to run. 'Rarebit', she called.

The two figures turned. 'Shush! Do you want to wake the dead?' Haro scolded. 'Well, Elya', he said, as she limped to the fire, 'so you decided to join us, after all!' The note in Haro's voice was unwelcoming, but in some way, Elya knew, he was oddly satisfied.

''lo', said Rarebit with a sickly grin. 'Got any food for a fella?'

'I don't know your name, young rabbit', scolded Trueme, hopping off Elya's shoulder, 'but I do think you could see that Elya has something to eat, before you ask for food for yourself'. The mouse was shaking with anger.

'Well, the little Poorme himself', Haro mocked. 'You've changed, indeed!'

'Trueme, if you please', said the mouse with dignity.

Haro sniffed. 'Come Elya', he said, ignoring the mouse. 'Sit here. You're welcome to a meal.'

Elya dropped on a log. The smell from the pot in front of her made her feel ill. 'What is it?' she asked.

'Herbs from the swamp', said Haro carelessly.

'The swamp? But aren't swamp herbs poisonous?' Trefoil had warned her about herbs which burnt the throat, made the head swirl, and left a nasty taste, as well as damaging health.

'Where did you get that idea? No, don't tell me. Trefoil! These herbs won't kill you, Elya, I assure you. In fact, they give unusual knowledge!'

73

A thought struck Elya. These were not ordinary herbs. Haro's eyes were strange, too bright for the usually self-contained hare. 'Haro', she said slowly, 'you didn't eat Dreevil's herbs?'

'Quite nice actually.' Haro crunched with enjoyment. 'Like some?'

Elya drew back. 'No thank you. Not Dreevil's herbs.'

Haro chuckled. 'One must live', he remarked.

Elya turned to Rarebit. 'Did you eat them, too?' she queried.

Rarebit would not look at her. 'Rarebit, they're dangerous. You know that!'

Haro was amused. 'Catch Rarebit going without his dinner', he said, 'but I can't say he enjoyed it much. That's why you want something else . . . to take the taste away, eh?'

The rabbit jumped up and went into the darkness, where the sound of retching rose into the night. 'No stomach for anything!' said the hare. 'Well, he'll survive. Now, tell me, Elya, why did you come here?'

Elya, her dark eyes round with earnestness, said: 'I want you to come back to Living Water Country'.

'Go back? Go back to Living Water Country? Elya, you can't be serious!'

'Of course I'm serious. You must know the swamp road is unhealthy as well as dangerous. Dreevil lives here, and Haro, look what happened to Krakik!'

The hare's ears curled with contempt. 'Really Elya, how tiresome you are! Krakik was stupid. You don't think I'd put myself into Dreevil's power, do you?'

Elya's clear gaze met his, and Haro turned away. 'Everyone wants you both to come back', coaxed Elya, softly. 'We love you, Haro.'

'Love? What's love?' Haro rose impatiently. His voice was harsh, his eyes hard. 'Love doesn't give knowledge or power. Sentimental rubbish! No, Elya, I'll never go back. Make up your mind about that!'

Elya sighed. She knew there was no use arguing. Haro's expression told her he would never be persuaded. 'Well, at least we'll come with you', she said at last. 'With four of us this way should be safer.'

The hare shrugged. 'Please yourself!' he said. 'I'm going to sleep, and I'd advise you to do the same, if you want to keep up with us. We have a long journey ahead tomorrow, even if it is easier than by way of Magis.' And without another word, he rolled himself into a blanket, and was sound asleep in an instant.

A few minutes later, Rarebit, looking pale and miserable, returned to the fire. He sat there shivering. Elya took out some tirips leaves and gave them to him. He snatched them greedily, and, without a word of thanks, began eating.

Taking out the bottle of water, she offered it to Trueme. He drank a little, and so did Elya. Hesitating, she offered the bottle to Rarebit, but he shook his head and chewed at the leaves. The colour had returned to his chubby cheeks, and he had become more cheerful. Elya, too, felt refreshed, but there was a pain around her heart that kept her from speaking. In silence, she wrapped herself and Trueme in the downy blanket she had been carrying, and tried to sleep.

'It's so quiet here', whispered the mouse. 'I don't even hear frogs!'

'M-mm', Elya murmured drowsily.

'It's funny Rarebit didn't want the living water. I wonder what he drinks.'

Elya was too tired to reply. 'It'd have to be swamp water, I suppose', mused Trueme. 'Ugh! No accounting for taste!' But Elya was asleep. In a few minutes the mouse, too, was dozing.

Trueme slept restlessly that night. Elya was weary beyond anything she had ever experienced, but peaceful slumber for her, too, was impossible. Once, she thought she heard someone creep toward them, but she was too tired to move, and she slept restlessly again.

When early morning came, Haro wakened them. Elya rose stiffly and shivered in the grey light, and Trueme crept sleepily to her side.

The hare urged them to hurry. 'I can't wait for sluggards', he said sharply. 'Get a move on, all of you.'

All signs of their presence had been removed. The pot with the stew had disappeared, and when Elya looked for the rest of the food she had brought with her, that had disappeared too. Only the bottle with the living water remained, and Rarebit, his round face cheerful, brushed his fur with a twig.

Elya and the mouse exchanged glances. They knew where the food had gone. Again Elya offered Trueme the living water, and they both drank. Haro looked on with a mocking smile.

Elya wrapped the bottle carefully in her blanket and said: 'We're ready, Haro'.

The hare leapt away. 'Follow me!' he said over his shoulder.

Elya had to run to keep up with him. Without her breakfast, she thought she would not be able to walk at all, but the living water gave her strength, and for some time, with Trueme at her heels, she was able to run beside the hare and the rabbit.

At last, however, she fell back. 'Haro, I'm not a hare!' she panted at last. 'Can't we stop for a minute?' She flopped at the side of the road.

Haro turned impatiently, and was about to say something, when the mouse screeched: 'You wicked creature! You don't care anything about your friend!'

Haro came back to them. 'Careful, Poorme', he said smoothly. 'Don't you be cheeky, or you might land in the cooking pot tonight.' He stretched out a paw, and the mouse jumped nervously away.

'Don't you touch him!' At the sight of Elya's angry, black eyes, the hare drew back. 'His name's Trueme now, and that's more than you are, Haro.'

Haro looked at her and wiggled his ears. He kept his voice even. 'Come, Elya. I'm not going to touch your precious mouse. Just as well we didn't go by way of Magis, or you would really have been in difficulty.'

Elya considered his remark. 'Perhaps the secret is to go gently, and not to rush into things', she said seriously.

Haro stared at her. 'Well, I'm not tired', he said. 'I've plenty of energy; so has Rarebit.'

'Ah, yes', squeaked the mouse, 'but he's had his breakfast, and so have you'.

Rarebit's ears blushed, but he opened wide his big blue eyes. Elya saw that all the innocence, if it had ever been there, had gone. They were wide, cunning eyes. 'Greedy, too!' she thought, but she looked at him with pity.

Rarebit cheekily returned her gaze for an instant, and then, in imitation of Haro, he said: 'One must live'.

Trueme opened his mouth to retort, but, before he could speak, Elya picked him up and put him on her shoulder. 'At least you can have a ride, Trueme', she said to divert him. 'Perhaps we could sing again as we did last night. It might help.'

Haro frowned. 'Of course we can, if you want to draw the attention of all the creatures in the swamp', he said. 'You're becoming a burden, Elya, and I really don't think I can be held back from this quest by anyone!'

Elya flushed. 'You invited me to come, Haro', she reminded him. 'And in the end I only came because I might be useful to you.'

'Thank you for nothing', snapped Haro. 'I can take care of myself. And what help are you if you make too much noise, I ask you!'

'I'm sorry. I didn't think', said Elya humbly.

'Yes, I'm sorry too', said Trueme, 'but only because we came. It seems to me that we're not really needed on this journey.'

Haro laughed. 'No. Not now that you're here!' And he laughed again.

'What do you mean?' asked Trueme, but the hare ran on, and they were forced to follow.

CHAPTER NINE

They stopped for lunch, later that day, near a bleak pool of water. Growing near its banks were some dried-up fruit trees and one dark tirips plant with shrivelled leaves. At least it was healthy food, and Elya was grateful. Haro had something in his pack which he chewed noisily, but he did not offer any of it to the others, not even to Rarebit. Rarebit was obviously disappointed, but was as silent as he had been for the whole journey.

'He's learnt better than to cross the hare', whispered Trueme, and Elya hushed him. She ate hungrily herself, and gathered extra fruit and leaves for the evening meal in case there was nothing else.

'It means we must carry it', she told Trueme, 'but we mightn't be able to keep up with Haro tomorrow, if we don't eat'.

She was beginning to think that she had been foolish to come on this journey, but how was she to know it would be useless? Another mouthful of the living water gave her energy, and quietly she waited for the hare to move.

The pace was unyielding and steady until evening. Haro grew grumpier as the day progressed, and Elya was frightened to talk to the mouse in case the hare shouted at her. When at last they came to the edge of the swamp, even Rarebit appeared tired and downhearted.

'Elya, I'm frightened', whispered Trueme. 'Unless they're under Dreevil's protection, no-one goes through the swamp. I thought we'd be going round the edge, nearer Magis, you know . . . but here! Dreevil'll be furious.'

'Haro says he can manage him', replied Elya, but she shivered.

A cold wet mist was rising around them. Elya imagined the sun had almost set, but she had not seen it for some hours, so she wasn't sure. The dim yellow light faded as they walked quickly along an overgrown path. Instead, the wavering mist surrounded them. For the last two days, as they had walked across the plains, there had been no sound. Here, the silence was cut from time to time with long drawn-out wails and cries of agony that echoed and re-echoed in the eerie stillness of the ragged swamp.

A dank odour of decaying leaves and vegetation filled their mouths and noses. The bushes, in thick, dark, straggling shapes, were silhouetted against the sky, and everywhere, rising from the evil-smelling mud beneath her feet, the cold steamy mist dampened everything, so that it rotted and fell apart at a touch.

'Like death', thought Elya. She tucked the mouse in her pocket. The smell of mould on rotting branches choked her. 'It's almost summer at home', she said to Trueme. The mouse snuggled against her.

Haro suddenly stopped and threw down his pack. 'We've come as far as we've planned', he said with satisfaction. 'Halfway to the mountains now. If we'd gone by way of Magis, we wouldn't even be a quarter of the way there.'

Cleverly, he rubbed two sticks together, and lit a fire. An unpleasant, smoking fire it was, for everything in the swamp was damp. Elya could see his face in the fast fading light. It was excited, triumphant, and looked slightly mad.

'Attaboy!' said Rarebit cheerfully. His chubby cheeks were glowing, though his eyes were tired.

Elya looked at the ugly roots of the misshapen trees which clawed the slimy earth. Thorn bushes, which grew so sparsely near Trefoil, grew here in wild abandon, reaching over gnarled trunks and matted branches. Prickly brambles pushed their long fingers through spikes of sodden grass.

Trefoil had told Elya that the trees and bushes of the swamp never communicated. In the beginning they had been frightened they would be overheard and punished, and afterwards, through lack of use, they became dumb. Trefoil had also said that, with difficulty, someone could change parts of the swamp. Looking around now, Elya thought change would be impossible.

She turned and stared at Haro. He had his blanket around his shoulders, and was gazing into the smoky fire, the hard lines of his hare's face deepening as he saw unseen pictures in the coals.

'Well, well', he said, turning to Elya. 'So, here it is at last, eh?'

Trueme put his tiny head out of Elya's pocket and, wrinkling his nose, squeaked: 'And what a place! Haro, you must be mad!'

Haro's good humour vanished, and his eyes, once so clear and wise, flashed red with anger. He wiggled his ears. 'Don't try me too far, little mouse', he said softly. His voice was dangerous.

'He's sick', thought Elya. 'No wonder, in this awful place!' She pushed the mouse back into her pocket, and gave him a tirips leaf to keep him quiet. Trueme, realising that she was warning him, ate his meal and did not show himself for some time. Elya took out the fruit and leaves they had gathered earlier, and half-heartedly began eating.

Haro again took something from his pack, and ate it without offering it to anyone.

Rarebit gobbled his own tirips leaves, and, when he had finished, sat staring at Elya, who tried to ignore him. She was about to pack the rest of the food away for the following day, when Rarebit's wide eyes made her change her mind. After all, he had been her friend! She offered him the small bundle to take his choice. Rarebit grabbed such a large handful that the mouse, emerging from Elya's pocket, squeaked indignantly.

'Crik, crik!' A frog jumped out of the mist and landed at Elya's feet.

'Krakik!' Elya could scarcely believe her eyes. 'Krakik! O Krakik!' She picked him up, and put him on her lap.

'Come to join the gang', said the frog, his broad smile widening until it took up his whole face.

Haro gave a start of surprise when he saw the frog. 'I understood you were dead', he snapped. He frowned.

Elya laughed delightedly. 'Krakik, how did you escape? I saw you being gobbled by Dreevil!'

'Tickled his belly', said Krakik. 'Can't bear to laugh, you know, but he did. Jumped off before he recovered.'

Elya giggled. 'O I wish I'd seen it!' she exclaimed, but instantly changed her mind. 'No I don't. I couldn't bear Dreevil. But what've you been doing all this time?'

'Went back to Saltbush Plains. Lived there for a while. Not settled, though. Decided to go to Lauristal. Heard about you from Chirrik. Saw you in the distance and followed.'

'And what about your singing?' asked Elya.

'Voice gone. Fright. Dreevil. Never mind. Better things in life!'

'So the voiceless frog wants to join the party to the Great Mountains', sneered Haro. Rarebit sniggered, and, seeing the hare was pleased with him for once, he broke into a loud guffaw and rolled in the dirty grass.

'Silly rabbit!' said Krakik with dignity, and turned to the hare. 'Not interested in mountains. Wanted to warn Elya.' He caught sight of Trueme, who was peeping wide-eyed from Elya's pocket. 'Hello!' he said.

'O Krakik, this is Trueme, the mouse', Elya said. 'He followed me too. What good friends you are!'

'If it's protection you want, it's a wonder your big friends didn't come', said the hare pleasantly, but there was venom in his face.

'Tricko and Rowlie have cubs in the spring', Elya said. 'They couldn't leave their families. In any case, Haro, you told us there was nothing to fear.'

'Of course not', said the hare. 'That's why I'm wondering at all the fuss.'

'Up to something', stated Krakik, looking at Haro's bland face.

'O come now, Krakik, your adventure has made you morbid. Settle down for the night . . . do! Elya is free to go back with you in the morning if she wishes. I'm not stopping her. She came of her own free will. I certainly don't need her.' Haro rolled his blanket around him as he spoke.

Krakik stared at him with unblinking eyes.

Elya had begun to prepare for the night. She made her friends comfortable, Krakik on a leaf, and the mouse in her pocket, and, after another mouthful of living water, she went to sleep herself.

Rarebit dodged around to pick up the forgotten tirips leaves. For a time he chewed at them. Haro moved over to look at the sleeping girl and her two small friends. There was a half smile on his face as he gazed at them, a smile that shone like a warning in the misty night. Rarebit saw it and smiled too, catching Haro's glance as he did so. The hare put his paw to his mouth to indicate silence, and Rarebit crept softly to the other side of the fire, stretched on the ground, and was soon asleep.

The group had been motionless for some time when the slithering sound of the snake near the edge of the clearing roused Haro. He sat up at once, and, glancing at the others to make sure they had not been disturbed, moved stealthily into the night.

Following the rustle of the snake as he slid along a faint path through the ugly thorn bushes, Haro came to a hillock of grass and mud rising above the surroundings in such a way that, while it appeared from a distance to be a large nest among the skeleton branches of dead trees, it was, in fact, a tower overlooking the land around. Haro, close behind the snake, entered a small cave of swamp reeds lit by a dim red light. He peered around, trying to discover the source of the light. He had several times wanted to ask the snake about it, but his courage always failed him, though he thought he could handle Dreevil in other ways.

Dreevil, amused, watched him. 'So, you have the child', he whispered at last. His eyes glittered.

'That was the agreement', murmured Haro. 'Elya's life for my safety through the swamp . . . and you owe me! Actually, there are three of them . . . four if you wish.'

'Four?' The monster's head rose in surprise. He looked suspiciously at Haro, who turned away in disgust from the snake's stinking breath. 'So you've been away on business? You wouldn't like to tell me about it, I suppose?' The snake paused, his coiled body still, his evil eyes on the hare's face.

Haro spoke slowly. 'Well, that mouse, you know . . . Poorme . . . the one who changed his name . . . he followed Elya. And an old friend of yours has had the cheek to risk his neck again . . . Krakik!'

Dreevil drew back his lips, and his eyes flashed. 'You have done well', he remarked.

'Too well to go unrewarded', said Haro with a smile, but his eyes were hard. 'You promised knowledge of good and evil . . . you must keep your promise!'

'You said four?' asked Dreevil.

'O Rarebit's become a bit of a nuisance lately. He'd be a good servant to you . . . and is worth . . . say, another branch of knowledge?'

Dreevil looked at the hare. 'You are, in your way, becoming accomplished in the field', he said smoothly.

Haro, smiling, nodded.

Dreevil's eyes sharpened suddenly, and, stretching his monster head, he peered at the camp fire in the distance. Haro swung round to see what had disturbed the snake. Krakik had woken, and was looking sleepily around him. Haro's blanket was bulging as though he were still in it, and the frog, after gazing at it for a long moment, put his head down again. The slow sound of frog snores rose in the night.

'Nearly as bad as his singing voice', remarked Dreevil.

'Is it decided Dreevil?' Haro asked impatiently.

'It is decided', hissed the snake.

'Well, Rarebit and I are leaving. I'll deliver him later . . . He'll be my surety for good payment', said Haro.

Dreevil inclined his head, but his evil eyes narrowed as he watched Haro climb cautiously down the hillock. It was as well Haro did not see that expression, or he might not have been so confident. He woke Rarebit, and together they stole down the putrid path deeper into the ugly, smelling swamp.

Dreevil watched them from his cave, and his face twisted in vengeful hatred.

CHAPTER TEN

Daylight struggled through the massed, thorny bushes, and Elya stirred. For a moment she tried to find her bearings. The sickly odour of mud and rotting branches rose around her, and she wrinkled her nose as she sat up. 'Pooh!' she exclaimed. 'It smells awful. Come on, Krakik and Trueme, it's time . . .' She stopped. There was no sign of the rabbit or the hare. 'Haro! Rarebit!' she called.

The frog woke with a start, and Trueme squeaked.

'Something the matter?' asked Krakik.

'O they've probably gone to get food or something', said Elya, but she felt afraid.

'Gone!' squeaked Trueme. 'They've gone! I knew it! I felt it in my fur! O I'm sorry, Elya. It's all my fault!' The mouse began to quiver.

'How can it be your fault?' asked Elya crossly. 'Now, don't start being Poorme again. We've enough trouble.'

The mouse's ears reddened, but instead of apologising he sat still and said nothing. His eyes showed his pain, however.

Elya noticed it, and at once she said, 'I'm sorry'. They both laughed.

Elya brushed her hair from her face. 'I'm sure they'll be back.'

'Packs are gone. No sign', remarked the frog.

Elya stood and looked around her. There was no sound of any living creatures besides themselves. She sat down on a rotting stump. Her face was white, and her breath came in choking gasps of fear.

'Come now', Trueme said gently. 'We must be brave. We'll find our way home, don't you worry.' He jumped on her shoulder, and patted her cheek with his tiny paw.

'Crick!' said the frog, which was the nearest thing he could do to a croak. 'Go home to Lauristal best, and Trefoil . . . Beautiful forest there . . .'

85

'And to Rowlie and Tricko and Chirrik', added the mouse.

Elya took a deep breath, and attempted to smile. 'We haven't any food, but we do have some of the living water', she said, and stretched out her hand for the leather bottle. 'O no!'

The three friends gazed at the upturned bottle. It was quite empty, and they saw, with horror, that Haro or Rarebit had poured the precious living water on the ground. A green patch of grass marked the spot, and three golden flowers lifted their heads in the dank ugliness, and gave three sparks of life to the dead, slimy surroundings.

'I can't leave them here', said Elya and, picking the flowers, she put them in the bottle.

Trueme stowed the few blades of grass in Elya's pocket, and, without looking at one another, the three friends faced toward Living Water Country. They began their journey homeward.

Elya felt hungrier than she had ever felt in her life. She was so weak that she had to move slowly and rest often. The black mist made her ill. It was not so much the swamp, though that was bad enough, but the thought of the treachery of her two friends made a tight band of pain around her heart. How could they do it? After all Living Water Country had done for them, how could they be so selfish? Now she knew the truth of Trefoil's teaching. 'Anyone can do anything', he had said. 'Everyone has free choice. I can choose to act, and the choice is mine . . . but if I choose bad things, I hurt myself and others. Good choices bring life.'

'O Trefoil, I wish you were here with me, and Lauristal too!' thought Elya.

Onwards they tramped, on and on and on.

'Not near Saltbush Plains', said Krakik at last.

Tears sprang to Elya's eyes. 'This is such a horrible place! The smell makes me sick!'

'And not only the smell', muttered Krakik. Trueme nodded.

'I know!' cried Elya. 'The flowers will help', and she shook them from the bottle to the palm of her hand. The perfume of living water rose in the foul air, and refreshed them. 'Here, Krakik, Trueme. I'll tie one to each of you with part of my dress — it's ruined anyway — and I'll wear one in my hair. We'll eat the blades of grass too.'

The two creatures looked so quaint with their flower hats that Elya began to smile again. She fastened the remaining flower in her hair and, for a time, they walked on merrily.

The mist-covered sun was high in the heavens when they stopped before a decaying tree. 'Krakik, we've been here before', Elya whispered through stiff lips.

'Crik! Not near Saltbush Plains', agreed Krakik, peering through the trees.

'We're back where we started!' wailed the mouse.

It was true. The small patch of green made by the living water was at their feet. They had been moving in a circle for hours!

As they looked at one another in dismay, Dreevil's monster head with its red, evil eyes rose from the bushes, and they heard his horrible chuckle.

'Dreevil!' shrieked Trueme, and hid in Elya's pocket, while Krakik hopped on her shoulder and faced the beast.

'No nearer, Dreevil!' he said.

The snake put back his head and roared with laughter. 'You poor little weevils', he said. 'What can you do against my power now?'

Elya, pale and trembling, turned to face him as Trefoil had told her so often. 'Go away, Dreevil', she said clearly.

For one moment Dreevil paused, but Elya, weakened by grief and exhaustion, felt her legs buckle. She fell to the ground.

Again the snake bared his fangs in wicked amusement. 'Hs-s-st!' he said, and his tongue flickered as he slid toward the fainting Elya. A stab of poison would render her helpless.

Little Trueme, galvanised to action, scampered out of Elya's pocket before Dreevil could see him, and darted at the snake's back just behind the neck. He bit deeply his sharp little teeth, crunching into the scaly skin. Dreevil drew back with a hiss of pain, and the monster head grew purple with fury. Krakik hopped back and forth in front of him, but as the snake turned his head, Krakik sprang toward the thorn bushes growing out of the slime of the swamp.

The snake, uncertain how to defend himself, flung himself round in circles. The mouse attacked again, this time on Dreevil's tail. That was a mistake, for the snake now had two of his victims in the same place. Though the frog tried to distract him by punching various parts of the long body, Dreevil ignored his ineffectual slaps, and turned his head toward Elya, who sat, dazed, watching him. With lips drawn and eyes ablaze, he swung forward, and encircled Elya with his dark, multicoloured coils. The foul stench of his breath made her lose consciousness.

At that precise moment, the breeze messenger of Living Water Country crossed the trees, bringing with him the fresh scent of the forest. The snake moved restlessly, but he was enjoying his victory and was in no hurry.

'One move from you, Trueme', he said, 'and she'll die instantly'.

The mouse froze, and Krakik stopped flapping.

For a minute they stared at one another. Dreevil threw back his head and laughed again.

Trueme was suddenly furious. 'You wretched creature!' he shrieked. 'Why don't you at least kill her quickly, and put her out of her misery?'

'She's not awake', said Dreevil smoothly, 'and I'm not ready yet. Besides, there is something for you to see.' Dragging Elya in his scaly coils, he moved toward a dark clump of trees where gruesome insects flew round and up and down without making a sound.

Krakik and Trueme, hoping even yet to release the child, yet afraid to attack in case the snake lost his temper, followed him.

'Horrible smell!' whispered Krakik. Dreevil turned his head and grinned with such evil joy that they shrank nearer the bushes.

And then they saw them. Rarebit, chubby cheeks puffed and eyes staring, was tied firmly, by strong grass reeds, to a tree. At the rabbit's feet, Haro lay flat on his back, also bound. The hare could only move his head. The two animals were barely alive. Long red weals and torn fur showed how they had fought a hard fight for freedom and lost.

As Krakik and Trueme stared, Elya moved weakly and opened her eyes. 'O!' she gasped. 'Poor Haro and Rarebit!'

Haro turned his head away, but Rarebit lifted his, and, for once, his strange blue eyes were full of tears.

'Five, I think', said Dreevil, giving Haro a flip with the end of his tail. 'You offered four for knowledge, and now you know. Five makes a good bargain.' He hissed his amusement.

Rarebit stared at Haro. 'You were usin' me!' he accused, his voice cracking.

Haro turned his head from Rarebit's surprised blue eyes. His hare's face was a sickly green. He closed his eyes.

'Run, Krakik', squealed Trueme suddenly, and scampered into the bushes. Krakik jumped after him. 'We'll get help', he called.

'O no you won't!' whispered Dreevil. He raised his head, and gave a long, loud hiss. Elya, terrified, shrank as far as possible from the evil red mouth.

The terrible swamp, which had seemed so lifeless, now began to move. From the murky earth, from every rotting tree stump, and from every reedy pool, snakes and crocodiles, poisonous insects, black, shiny, nameless creatures of every shape and size, began to crawl into the open. There was no sound from the slithering, relentless mob. Krakik and Trueme had no hope; they were pushed back to the place where Dreevil lay.

'You wanted to know why I am taking so long to kill?' he mocked. 'Now you see. I have many servants who will enjoy this feast — with the eyes — even if they don't eat.' And for the third time, his hissing evil laugh rang out in the swamp.

CHAPTER ELEVEN

Meanwhile, the breeze whistled across the Saltbush Plains, flowed over the great forest, rustled leaves, and whispered his message through tree branches and shivering grasses. Birds and animals listened while the word flew up, up, up to the sky, till it reached the stars and made them tremble.

Everyone heard Elya's cry. It rang in the clear night air as though she stood among them: 'Save us!' No-one queried that call. In the heart of the tree, in the very depths of the pool, in the sound of the rushing river, a sword pierced, a sword of sorrow, and every voice, in one accord, made response. 'Save her! Save the child!'

The mighty Magis roared and rushed. Silver spears rent the black sky, and a clash of thunder rumbled and growled over the forest. Trees trembled; flowers folded their petals and hid their gentle faces close in their leaves; animals scuttled for shelter; birds hid in the trees and crevices of rocks; all creatures felt the wrath of the gathering storm, and rejoiced in it.

Deep in the swamp, Dreevil was trying to decide who would be his first victim. His coils lay in an iron grip around the motionless Elya, but his eyes flickered from Haro to Rarebit, to Trueme and Krakik, and back again.

Suddenly the sky split over swamp, plains, and forest alike. Rain fell. Surprised, Dreevil loosened his coils for a moment, and Elya sprang from his grasp. She ran heedlessly, and fell choking into the slimy mud among the bushes. With all her remaining strength, she pushed herself away from Dreevil.

At the same moment, the roar of Magis made the snake turn his head. The river gushed over rocks, spilt over ravines and valleys, swelled his waters in great foaming waves. There was a moment of utter confusion in the clearing. The horrible slimy creatures pushed and struggled in their efforts to find shelter. They fought and kicked; they twisted and writhed; they screamed and shrieked.

Krakik and Trueme dashed forward and renewed their attack on the snake, but he slithered away under a rotting tree and, leaving his wicked friends to fend for themselves, found his way back to his hillock.

Rising swiftly, Magis left his banks in torrential streams. He poured through the swamp from the east, tossed his waters over the thorn bushes and trees, and swamped every plant and ugly bush. Nothing would be overlooked in his search for Elya. Lit by flashing lightning, his gleaming waters guided him on his way.

The crawling, vicious creatures were scattered. Only a few escaped. Magis caught most of them in his surging anger, and tossed them among the rocks on his eastern bank, where they remained cold and shivering for many days. He ignored them, and continued his search.

At last, he found Elya with her two small friends. Lifting the three of them in his strong current, he carried them far away from Dreevil's putrid land.

When they were safe, the river bore down on Haro and Rarebit. The tree to which Rarebit was tied crashed into the water, and a branch severed his bonds. Rarebit struggled to lift Haro to the trunk, but Magis swept them both away, and battered them relentlessly against the rocks of his own path to the Great Mountains until they were limp. He released them at last. At midnight, Haro, at last free from the reed ropes that had bound him, crawled sullenly from the water to the dry land of Saltbush Plains. Rarebit followed him, but as soon as they reached firm land, without a word the rabbit turned and limped in the opposite direction from the path Haro was taking. The rabbit hid in a hollow tree stump at the edge of the forest, but it was to be a long time before he showed his chubby face at the pool.

Haro made a burrow in Saltbush Plains. He would not forget this night, but, stripped of his pride, he would never go back to Living Water Country, nor would he ever trust Dreevil again. He would live a sad and lonely life between good and evil.

As the storm cleared, Magis circled Dreevil's hillock. The river wondered what he could do to teach the wretched snake a lasting lesson. It was not in Magis's nature to kill, and he knew that Dreevil, steeped in evil, would never change.

Suddenly he chuckled; stars twinkled, and the moon smiled. Dreevil, in his reedy cave lit by the red light, heard the sound and raised his head.

Gently, Magis swirled and twirled, twisted and rippled. The snake, terrified, circled his scaly body with the water, and followed each movement with his glittering eyes until he was giddy.

All night Magis circled, and all night Dreevil, sick and faint, circled with him.

At dawn, Magis receded, but round the hillock he left behind him a lake of crystal water that he would continually renew through the centuries till the dawn of time in the Great Mountains. The putrid hillock, with its only occupant, was the one point above water.

Every time Dreevil wanted to leave his hillock in future, he would have to swim through the shining water of the White Lake, a fate worse than death for this evil creature. If he tried to live elsewhere, he would have to leave behind all the spells and horrors he had collected for centuries. They would never survive passing through living water, and if he left them with no-one to guard them, others could find them and become more powerful than he.

Dreevil cursed Magis with all the strength of his evil spirit, but he had no power against Magis. Ill and wretched in the cold dawn, the snake hissed his despair, and burrowed deeply into the slime of the hillock to nurse his defeat.

Magis, in the meantime, drew Elya and her friends from the crevice where he had hidden them, and passed on through the warmer waters of Living Water

Country. Tumbling the frog and the mouse into Lauristal's clear waters as he passed, he swept Elya onwards, rocked her gently in his waters, and finally placed her softly on the sand before rushing and foaming into the sea for his morning bath. Elya slept.

Seagulls squawked in the heavens, and dropped to look at her. Birds twittered in nearby trees. The sand grew white in the daylight; morning mist lifted, and the sea waves ebbed and flowed in a rhythm of life. The perfume of saltbush and pine, and the fresh, tangy smell of the sea filled the air as the sun rose and dressed the world in gold, while the rosy sky gave promise to a new day.

Back at the pool, Krakik and Trueme told their stories over and over to an entranced audience of forest creatures who had gathered to hear the news. Together they awaited the child's return. Excitement grew.

'Changes coming', said Krakik at last, and Trefoil nodded.

'She is ready for the call', he said, and his old branches trembled with joy. 'A choice and her sad experiences have matured her. We shall not keep Elya much longer.'

'Why not?' demanded Trueme.

Lauristal smiled at the mouse. 'Everyone must change to grow', she said. 'To sit still and refuse to answer a call means stagnation.'

'Why?' asked Trueme. 'Why can't she stay as she is, and be happy?'

'That would be following the selfish call . . . like Haro and Rarebit. It is the inner call that matters', said Trefoil. The forest creatures were silent.

'I think I need lessons', said Trueme. 'You'd like that, Krakik, wouldn't you?'

'Crik! Crik! Delighted!' Krakik's smile spread from one side of his face to the other. 'Early education lacking. Need to make up before too late.'

'You can join the three of us', said Naylor, and looked down from his horse's height at the two small friends.

'Quite a mixture!' Trefoil's branches cracked, and everyone laughed.

Rowlie stretched; his muscles rippled. 'Will Elya need company on her way back from the sea?' he asked hopefully.

'It is better to leave her.' The tree was quietly firm. 'She has Magis . . . and the Master.'

All eyes turned to him.

Tricko stood. 'So that's why you're so sure about the call! What a secretive old tree you are, Trefoil!' His brown eyes snapped with amusement, and he saluted Trefoil with his bushy tail.

'She will come back for a time to prepare for her journey by way of Magis', continued the tree. 'The Master has called her to the Great Mountains . . . to *his* way of knowledge. He is pleased with our teaching.'

'She's coming, coming, coming!' warbled Chirrik, and flew excitedly to perch on Trefoil's branches.

Elya, clad in a bright robe, with black hair flowing, and grace in every step, walked into the clearing from the south. Her face was alight with love and joy, and there was laughter in her dark eyes. The wayward child had vanished, and in her place stood a courageous young woman, standing straight and tall, a loving and lovable human being. She gazed on her friends without speaking.

A great hymn of thanksgiving rose in the forest, from the smallest insect to the largest animal, from every tree and flower and breeze. Lauristal rippled; Trefoil raised his branches to the sky; and Magis rushed past in joyful abandon.

The awesome moment was broken at last by the cheeky Chirrik. 'Time for tea, tea, tea!' she chirped.